Playin' Cop

Sign up at *www.LizKellyBooks.com*
to be alerted when new books are released.

PLAYIN' COP

HEROES OF HENDERSON: PREQUEL

Liz Kelly

Published by Kelly Girl Productions
©Copyright 2013 Liz Kelly
Cover design by Tammy Kearly

ISBN: 978-0-9889838-7-8

For more information on the author and her works, please see
www.LizKellyBooks.com

Dedicated with love to
Harry & Jody Ford
One of the world's great romantic couples.

CHAPTER ONE

New Year's Eve - Noon

"So how many laws are we about to break?"

Duncan James couldn't help but smile. Sitting shotgun in his best friend Brooks Bennett's police cruiser, he'd been mulling over that question himself ever since they'd pulled off the road, lying in wait for the target of their bet. He glanced over at Brooks' long, lanky frame comfortable in the police uniform after six years on the job. "Why are you asking me?" Duncan said. "You're the cop."

"And you're the lawyer." Brooks folded his arms over his chest, turned his head and allowed a broad and engaging grin to expand under his mirrored sunglasses and short cropped curly bronze hair. He chomped on his gum a few times before admitting, "Nah, we're in the clear. Mr. Devine gave us his blessing. He knows darn well his baby Annabelle needs to slow herself down a peg on these back roads. You met Harry Devine about a month ago at the Club, remember? Same night we arranged this bet."

"And I'm looking forward to meeting his baby Annabelle who has curled you and Vance around her little finger. This is going to be like taking candy from a baby. And I'm talking about you and Vance, not Miss Devine."

"You, my fancy friend, are about to meet your comeuppance."

Duncan shook his head and glanced out at the pine trees surrounding them. His golden eyes narrowed at the artfully tousled hairstyle he saw reflected in the side-view mirror. He supposed he was fancy compared to his buddies. Neither of them would ever spend any real money on a haircut or shoes or be caught dead wearing a cashmere coat. But this entire week between Christmas and New Year's had been unseasonably cold for North Carolina and he wanted to look official without actually impersonating an officer. "It just can't be that hard to give a woman a speeding ticket. Seriously. I know you've said she's a hottie and all. But it's your job to give tickets. And between you and Vance, you've stopped this woman how many times?"

"Well it's not that easy when you've known the girl all your life. Maybe it will be easier for you."

"Damn right it's gonna be easier for me. I don't care how hot she is, or if she pouts her lips and claims she's racing home to a dying relative. This Annabelle Devine is going down. And you and Vance will be paying my bar tabs for all of next year."

Brooks' grumbled curse was cut off by the hearty sound of Vance's voice coming over the police scanner. "Just spotted Baby D looping around the exit ramp off 85 revving her engines and heading for home."

"Affirmative," Brooks responded. Then he threw a mischievous grin at Duncan. "Buckle up. It's show time," he said as he started the cruiser. They waited patiently until the custom-made, wide-bodied, motor roaring, fire-engine red Camaro flew by.

"Holy shit," Duncan whispered.

Brooks pulled out in hot pursuit, spraying gravel as his tires fought for purchase. "What kind of a woman drives a car like that?" Duncan breathed. He tightened his seatbelt as Brooks hit the siren and they began to gain speed. The Camaro was nothing but an elusive red dot at the end of Duncan's vision. "How the hell are we going to catch her?"

"We'll catch her. Eventually. I know where she lives." Brooks punched the gas pedal.

Duncan was thrown back in his seat, but he kept his eyes trained on the dot on the horizon. "How fast is she going?" He glanced over at the speedometer. "Holy hell, how fast are *we* going?"

"Just sit back and enjoy the ride."

It took a good ninety seconds for the cruiser to start gaining ground. The brief flash of brake lights and gradual slow-down indicated when the driver realized they were behind her. Eventually, a pale, slender arm ventured out the window, waving them around.

"Does she think you're heading to an emergency? Not pulling her over?'

"She knows I'm pulling her over."

"Ah. Her tactics already at work, I see."

Eventually the muscle-bound Camaro slowed to a stop and they pulled up behind it on the shoulder of the road. Duncan could not take his eyes off the souped-up machine and imagined the driver with tattoos and body piercings, dyed black hair and skull and crossbones jewelry. None of which he found particularly hot. This was going to be a cakewalk.

Brooks threw the car into park and said, "Okay Dunc, you're on. The bet is you have to give Annabelle a full-blown speeding ticket. No letting her off with just a warning to make yourself her hero. If you manage that, we pick up your bar tab anytime we're together over the next year."

"Here and in Raleigh," Duncan clarified.

"Here and Raleigh." Brooks nodded. "In addition, if she meets Vance at the courthouse and actually pays this fake ticket, whatever money changes hands you get to keep."

Imagining how the scene was going to play out, Duncan nodded, cleared his throat and reached for the door handle. Then he stopped. "Give me your glasses." Brooks handed them over and Duncan exited the car in one graceful move. He donned the mirrored shades, turned up the collar of his coat and pulled a pair of black leather gloves out of his pocket. He squared his shoulders and applied his gloves like he was strapping on a gun belt and heading for a showdown.

As he approached, a flurry of activity caught his attention through the Camaro's rear window. *What the hell is she doing? Brushing her hair? Putting on lipstick?* As if he were going to fall prey to her heavily mascaraed feminine wiles. Even if body piercings were his thing, he had a bet to win. A very simple bet. All he had to do was give the speed demon a ticket. In his mind, he was already regaling their fraternity brothers at NC State's next Homecoming about besting Brooks and Vance.

Duncan rapped his knuckles on the driver's side window like he'd done this a million times. When the electric window slid down, he put both his gloved hands on the sill of the door and leaned down to get a good look at the driver.

"Danica Patrick, I presume?"

Annabelle Devine's endorsement-ready smile broke wide as she tossed the curling ends of her *Pretty Woman* mass of red hair over one shoulder. Her spontaneous laugh drew Duncan in, and when she pulled off her designer shades, her bright brown eyes and fresh-faced beauty shocked the hell out of him. Where was the nose ring? She was nothing like he'd pictured.

"And you must be Officer Friendly," she drawled.

Quick-witted too!

An unbidden grin crept to life as Duncan leaned in a little closer. "Good a name as any, I suppose," he said, his brain starting to panic. He'd planned to play Bad Cop, but suddenly he found he didn't have it in him. His libido argued that Officer Friendly could give tickets too. "Do you have any idea how fast you were going?"

Annabelle placed one manicured hand over his right glove. "Now, Officer. My daddy is waitin' on me at home just up the road not five minutes from here. And if you'll indulge me, I'll tell you that he and Mother throw a big New Year's Eve ball every year at the Country Club and he relies on me to help him oversee the set-up. Mother can get a little over-zealous with the decor, making it just a teensy bit gaudy, if you know what I mean. Daddy relies on me to be the go-between. I'm sure you can understand. If I'm able to play my part, the entire family arrives at the ball in a good mood and there are no awkward moments for our guests. Now," she said, tilting her head and batting her long, long lashes, "I know you don't want me to be late and disappoint my daddy."

Duncan found her Southern accent charming. And her evasive maneuvers entertaining.

"Miss Devine." When the sparkle in her eyes shifted from amusement to curiosity, he said, "Yes, I know your name. In fact, you've become rather infamous. So infamous that it might be more appropriate to call me *Special Agent* Friendly, because I've been called in to make sure the Henderson Police Department ends the year on a high note."

"Excuse me?"

"You seem to have friends in high places, Miss Devine. And although you've been pulled over on this very road many times during the last twelve months, you've never actually been given a speeding ticket. Isn't this true?"

Annabelle patted his gloved hand. "Oh, you misunderstand, I'm sure. I may have been stopped by Lieutenant Evans or Lieutenant Bennett once or twice, but that wasn't about speeding tickets. That was about catching up."

"Catching up?"

"You know how it is in a small town," she went on. "I live an hour away in Raleigh now, but I was born and raised in Henderson, just like Lieutenants Evans and Bennett. In fact, they are both my sister Tess' age. Do you know either of my sisters, Special Agent Friendly?"

Duncan chuckled at the name. "I don't believe I've had the pleasure."

"Well, I'd be happy to introduce you. Vance and Brooks like to pull me over whenever I'm coming to town so they can hear all about what my sisters are doing. My life isn't very exciting, as you can probably tell, but Tess and Grace are living fabulously exciting lives. Tess is an actress on Broadway. I mean who-the-heck in Henderson has ever done that? And Grace, well she works for the FBI and I'd tell you more but then…you know…."

"You'd have to kill me."

"Exactly," she grinned, tapping his hand again. "I like you, Special Agent Friendly. Seems to me you'd know how to have a good time."

And he was more than certain that the very quick and clever third Devine sister knew how to have a very good time. "I'll take that as a compliment."

"Please do. So you see, I may have been stopped a couple of times, but it was all very social. No tickets needed."

"Are you telling me this is the one and only time, all year, you've flown down this road in this fine piece of machinery and created a sonic boom?"

Annabelle sighed deeply and looked around the interior of her car, caressing the leather of the steering wheel. "She is a beauty, isn't she?" she asked, returning her gaze to Duncan's face.

Duncan couldn't help it. He stared directly into Annabelle's eyes and told the truth. "Never seen anything prettier."

Annabelle ducked her head shyly and bit her lip. With her pale skin, rosy cheeks, pearl stud earrings and rose-scented perfume, she was the epitome of lady-like grace. Duncan felt the urge to pull off his glove and tangle his hand in all that red hair. From there, it was easy to imagine tilting her head and bringing her lips up to meet his.

Whoa. Head in the game, man.

A bit of panic floated around his chest. With thoughts like that this bet was going to go south on him fast. He looked back toward Brooks in an effort to fight the distraction caused by the dichotomy of the seriously pimped-out muscle car and the elegant, astute Southern belle sitting behind the wheel.

He cleared his throat, stood up straight and got back to business. "Your seat belt is fastened," he noted. "The car is obviously in good condition. Is there any sort of emergency I need to know about?"

Annabelle stuttered. "You mean…other than my daddy?"

"License and registration, please."

"Seriously?" Annabelle had the audacity to look appalled.

"Miss Devine. It's noon. Your father's party starts at what time? Eight o'clock? I'm afraid that does not constitute an emergency."

He loved how she hesitated just a moment before leaning over and opening her glove compartment. Clearly, capitulating was not sitting well with her. He almost had to smile, deducing she was too well-brought-up to put up much more of a fight when she was so clearly in the wrong. He watched the cascade of red hair fall over her shoulder and how she tucked it behind her ear as she daintily handed him a small leather portfolio. She glanced up at him briefly, then back to the portfolio. "Everything should be in order."

"Thank you. I'm going to put your information into our computer to see just how many social chats you've had over the last year."

"Is this really necessary?" she asked meekly. Obviously, the fear of a big fat speeding ticket was finally seeping in.

"Just sit tight. I'll be back in a couple of minutes and get you on your way to Daddy."

With a distraught little pout, Annabelle said in a small voice, "I appreciate that, Officer."

Duncan's heart twisted. He'd never felt more like a bully. He tapped her portfolio against his other glove. Standing there. On the brink. Teetering.

The only sound registering was that of his heart pounding in his ears.

Finally, he turned toward Brooks and the patrol car, issuing orders to his legs. *Right, left, right, left…that's it. Keep going. All the way back to safety.* He didn't trust himself around pretty pouty baby Annabelle for one more minute. He opened the door and launched himself inside.

"How'd it go?" Brooks asked.

Duncan turned his entire body to face his so-called friend. "You have got to be kidding me!" he launched. "Hot? A hottie? That's how you describe a *work of art?*"

"A work of what?"

"You're an idiot, you know that? You and Vance. You two had me thinking Annabelle Devine was a—I don't know…the kind of girl Vance likes to pick up late at night at Spanky's. That girl," he said pointing out the windshield. "That girl is drop-dead gorgeous. The quintessential Southern belle. She's charming, she's witty…my God, she's just as well-bred as she can be, physically, socially and mentally."

Brooks started to talk but choked on his own words as he heard the last part of Duncan's tirade. Sputtering, he coughed out, "What the hell did you just say?"

"She's the one. She's the one I'm going to marry."

The two men just stared at each other. Duncan pissed off, and Brooks looking like he'd swallowed a lizard.

Finally Duncan broke the silence. "How much is the ticket?"

Brooks' mouth just opened and closed under wide, stunned eyes.

"The fine, you son-of-a-bitch. What's the fine for traveling at the speed of light?"

"Three hundred dollars."

Duncan moved his head rapidly in a set of short nods. "Give me the ticket book." As he took it, he glanced out the windshield to find Annabelle climbing out of her vehicle and heading toward them. It was December 31, colder than should ever be allowed in North Carolina, and his future bride was dressed in a tiny slip of white material that barely covered her torso, much less her arms and legs.

Duncan looked over at Brooks with a roll of his eyes. "Been nice if you had told me she was insane." He leapt out of the squad car and rushed forward, taking his coat off as quickly as possible.

"I know it gets hot in those race cars, Danica," he joked as he reached her at the halfway mark, "but it's twenty-eight degrees out here in this crazy cold snap and you're dressed for a summer wedding." He flung his coat behind her and then brought it up over each of her bare shoulders. Grabbing a lapel in each hand, he pulled them together to securely wrap her killer body inside the warmth of the thin, soft cashmere. He knew it was a killer body because she'd stumbled forward as he wrapped her up, landing firmly against him from chest to thigh. His higher brain congratulated him on his dumb luck. He could not have planned this any better. His legs were slightly apart and her pale pink heels nestled right in between his loafers. Instinctively his arms went around her and rubbed up and down her back, trying to warm her as they stood together in the elements.

Appearing a bit flustered, Annabelle looked down at the lack of space between them and then up into his eyes. He was all of six feet, but the look she gave him made him feel a helluva lot taller. "I know I look ridiculous, but there is an explanation," she whispered.

"There is? I'd love to hear it. First, let's get you back into your car. You can roll down the window a couple of inches and tell me."

Now Duncan stood outside without a coat, but at least he had on a sweater, button-down and wool pants. He crossed his arms over his chest and shuffled from foot to foot. Annabelle turned on her car, cranked up the heat, then rolled down her window and passed his coat back to him. He quickly put it back on.

"You warm enough in there? Roll the window back up. Just leave it open a crack so I can hear you." She did as she was told.

"I just came from a photo shoot for work," she explained, her chin slanted up so her voice would carry out of the car. "We had to wear white."

Duncan shook his head like he was trying to clear cobwebs. "And that explains the lack of a coat, hat, gloves and scarf how?"

"Well, clearly I was not anticipating stopping between there and my parents' house."

"Clearly." Duncan took a deep breath. "Okay, Miss Devine—"

"Please, call me Annabelle. That was awfully nice of you to lend me your coat." Annabelle glanced down at her lap, and after a moment turned her head to the side and smiled at him. "Sort of makes you an officer *and* a gentleman."

Duncan's heart skipped two beats. "My pleasure…Annabelle."

There was a moment then. A long, slow, moment that Duncan would reflect back on in private. A moment when the weather and the car and the bet with his buddies all evaporated and nothing was left except the two of them, smiling at one another. Everything went blank. So when the thought entered his head, it came like the roar of thunder.

I've found you.

Annabelle broke the spell first, shyly glancing down and then back up. "Is that Brooks Bennett in the car with you? I think if we could just get him involved, he may be able to help sort all this out."

"Brooks?" Duncan leaned down as close as he could to the window. He lowered his voice indicating the game had changed. "Brooks can't help you now, darling. This is between you and me."

Annabelle's eyes went wide.

Duncan stood and whipped out the ticket book he'd shoved into his coat pocket. He flipped it open and wrote her name. "Let's make this as quick and painless for you as possible. Like ripping off a Band-Aid. Being as it's December 31, and I know the city of Henderson would love to have your money in their coffers before they close the books out for the year, if you pay your fine in cash at City Hall before they close today, Lieutenant Bennett and I will arrange for there to be no court date or any reporting back to your insurance company. No points on your record either. As a courtesy. For helping out the city. It can't get much cleaner than that."

Annabelle angled her pretty little head at him and rolled her eyes. "A courtesy. For helping out the city." She sighed and checked her watch. "The bank should still be open. How much is the ticket?"

"Three hundred dollars." He slid the ticket through the opening in the window.

"Three hundred dollars? You've got to be kidding me. For three hundred dollars you should be giving me a police escort to and from City Hall."

"That can be arranged."

Annabelle held the ticket in front of her, saying under her breath, "For this kind of money I could have bought myself an escort for the party tonight." And then her head shot up and she paused for a second before turning toward him, eyes determined. She lowered the window halfway. "Look. I am not going to be the one stuck kissing Lewis Kampmueller!"

"What do you have against—"

"I'll pay your ridiculous ticket, in cash, before five o'clock under one condition. You be my date tonight."

"Tonight?" Duncan took a step back from the car and rubbed a gloved hand over his chin. *Be cool. Do not blow this.* "Annabelle Devine. Do I look like the kind of guy who doesn't have a date lined up for New Year's Eve?"

"Well, do you?" she challenged. "Frankly, I don't care. If this little fiasco is costing me three hundred dollars, I'm going to get my money's worth. You're Officer Friendly, you have a duty to serve and protect. Break your date. I have to be there early, so meet me at the Henderson Country Club at eight. I want full service in return for my cooperation with these shenanigans. It all sounds very fishy to me. "

"Well now," Duncan said, dropping his voice and making it full of promise, "Officer Friendly, at your service. Pay your fine before the close of business today and I'll provide as much service as you can handle."

Annabelle sucked in a breath and blinked several times.

Duncan turned and walked away. Grinning.

He heard her window slide down further and then Annabelle shouting, "Don't you want to know the address?"

He continued to walk toward the squad car. "I'm a cop. With an iPhone. I'll find it."

"Do you own a tux?" she shouted back.

That stopped him in his tracks. He turned around slowly, incredulous. "What? Do I look like I was born in a barn?" That had her smiling, waving him off and turning around to fasten her seat belt.

Duncan headed back to Brooks and the squad car. That, he thought, had gone very, very well. He slid into the passenger seat and asked Brooks, "How fast can this thing get us to Raleigh and back?"

"Why? What the hell is going on?"

"I need to pick up my tux."

Brooks broke into a broad grin as he started the car and spun out on two wheels, turning them around. "So. The Keeper of the Debutantes, huh?" He glanced at Duncan, then shook his head. "Man, I did not see that coming."

CHAPTER TWO

Annabelle made sure to drive the speed limit the rest of the way home. The thought of dishing out three hundred dollars on the heels of her Christmas bills sat heavy in her stomach like that god-awful fruitcake Aunt Helen forced her to eat last weekend. She pulled into the large circular driveway of her family home—an impressive red brick, white-trimmed and black shuttered two-story colonial with a wing off each side. Standing atop the brick landing just outside the opened front door was her entire family.

Brooks must have called them.

Her father, Harry Devine, stood a head taller than the women surrounding him. His dark hair had started to fade into a distinguished gray, but his handsome features kept him looking like a man too young to have so many grown daughters. His sharp eyes of deep, dark brown were the origin of the Devine Brown-Eyed Girls, for he had passed them on to each of his three daughters. He was gregarious and kind-hearted, and had more fun at his annual New Year's Eve party than anyone because he loved to dance—and he was good at it. Every woman invited wanted to dance with him.

Her mother, Jody, stood waving Annabelle in, petite and pretty as always. Honey blonde like Tess, but with sea blue eyes which all her daughters envied. Her ever-present three carat diamond studs glistened in the sunlight.

On either side of her mother stood the two best big sisters a girl could have. She was so proud of Tess and her famous Broadway voice that she could easily overlook the whole bossing around thing she would inevitably do. At least for a few days. And Grace, their superstar athlete, was the best keeper of secrets and hardly ever pinged Annabelle on her head while she was reading anymore.

Annabelle had to laugh in spite of herself as they all started jeering and applauding the moment they saw her. It was like doing the walk of shame in her car. She had to drive by them all before reaching the paved pull-off where she parked. She took a deep breath and sighed heavily before getting out to face the music.

She held up her hands in surrender. "I know, I know. Wow, good news must really travel fast." She managed to smooth the sides of her short shift before Grace, who had bounded down the steps laughing, wrapped her up in a big bear hug.

"Oh, it's a big day when the law finally catches up to my baby sister," Grace said, turning them both toward the rest of the family. She kept an arm firmly around Annabelle's waist as they walked. "Finally you weren't able to flirt your way out of a ticket. Henderson's finest must be upping their game."

"Well, I suppose an FBI agent would think so." Annabelle stopped short. "You didn't set this up, did you?"

Grace laughed, her light brown bangs falling into her eyes. She tucked them back and started walking. "Never," she vowed. "Blood is thicker than water, after all. I've always got your back."

"Just like I'll always sing your praises," Tess added, as the girls approached the rest of the family.

Annabelle squealed and threw her arms around Tess in a tight embrace. "Well, if you're the one doing the singing, at least it will sound good," she said into her sister's neck. They parted slightly so each one could look at the other. "I'm so glad you were able to get home. Grace and I missed you over Christmas and the New Year's Eve ball would be absolutely no fun without you."

"You mean there wouldn't be as much fodder for the gossip mill if I didn't show my face."

"Not at all," Annabelle replied sincerely. "You're Henderson's shining star. Our golden girl. And you're gonna find everyone standing solidly in your corner as the news of your divorce breaks." Annabelle could see the doubt in her sister's eyes, along with lingering hurt and regret. She leaned in and kissed her cheek. "Trust me on this. All is well. You'll see." And then she stepped back and with a victorious grin said, "Besides, since I won't be the one Lewis Kampmueller gets to slobber all over at midnight, I'm sure Grace appreciates you offering some competition."

"What?" Grace shouted.

"I thought you weren't bringing anyone from Raleigh," said Jody.

Annabelle's eyes shifted quickly to her dad, then she threw an arm over her mother's shoulders to usher her inside. "Well…there seems to be a silver lining to this whole speeding ticket debacle. Apparently, for three hundred dollars, I am not only helping out the city of Henderson, but I've hired myself an escort as well."

"Holy hell," her father muttered.

Ignoring that, Annabelle stepped over the threshold saying, "Somebody pour me a cocktail and I'll tell you all about it."

Grace and Tess took a look at each other and burst out laughing. "Oh, this is gonna be good."

⟨ᴥᴥᴥᴥ⟩

Later, when all the catching up was done between the sisters and their mother, and each of them had shuffled off to take care of various errands before the party, Annabelle found her father in his library watching a football game. "Which bowl is this?" she asked, coming in and sitting down on the leather ottoman in front of him.

"The Nissan-Hair Remedy For Men.com-Fly Your Bags for Free or some such nonsense, Bowl. I swear to God. Give me the Rose or the Sugar or even the Fiesta Bowl. But all this sponsorship stuff can make a fan nutty."

"I hear ya. Who do you have in the Orange Bowl?'

"I took West Virginia and the points." Annabelle turned toward him in shock. "Don't look at me like that. I may be Tar Heel born and Tar Heel bred and on and on until I'm dead," he said, making a mockery of the Carolina fight song, "but my money has no allegiance whatsoever."

Annabelle turned back to the TV. "I hear that," she mumbled.

Her dad sprang forward, putting a hand on her shoulder. "What? You didn't take Carolina either?"

She turned and gave him a withering look. "Between you and me, it's a total fluke that they won the ACC. The Mountaineers are going to roll all over them." She turned back to the TV. "And it's gonna hurt."

"I hear that."

They watched a few uneventful plays in silence.

Annabelle finally glanced at her watch. "Do I need to...."

"All taken care of, sugar bee."

She turned her head and asked, "You talk to Brooks or Vance?"

"Vance. He was on his way to City Hall to wait for you. Apparently Brooks had to make an urgent run to Raleigh." That got a smile out of Annabelle. Her father went on. "I told Vance we'd settle up tonight." She nodded at that. Then she got up and came over to kiss her father's cheek.

"Thanks for setting all that up for me, Daddy. You were right. I think I just might like this Officer Friendly."

Her father grabbed her hand as she started to walk away. "His name is Duncan James, sugar bee. And it wasn't long after I met the boy that I thought he might be perfect for my Annabelle. After all, I know just how picky you are. He's got good manners, a firm handshake and solid eye contact. Word is he works hard, but is no stick in the mud. He lives in Raleigh so he can go home to his own damn place after a date. And although he made the poor decision to go to NC State, we won't hold that against him because he got his law degree at Carolina."

Annabelle laughed.

"You go have fun tonight and see what you think." Annabelle nodded and started to walk away. "Gotta be better than swapping spit with old Lewis Kampmueller."

"I hear that," she heartily agreed.

CHAPTER THREE

On the outskirts of Henderson stood a long and dreary ranch-style house that would only be called a fixer-upper by an optimist. Good thing Brooks Bennett had his share of optimism in spades, because he'd been its proud owner for six months now. Time enough for him to pull down all the wallboard and strip the thing to its studs, opening the kitchen, dining and living room areas to make one big great room. New wallboard was now up, taped, sanded and ready for paint. But all his furniture was crammed into one of the three bedrooms down the hall. The place was clean for a construction site and had a working refrigerator filled with beer—which seemed to be the only requirement for the four men who made do by sitting in three beach chairs and on top of a cooler right in the middle of Brooks' new great room.

"No problem," said Lewis. "Staying with your parents will be a heck of a sight better than this dump. Duncan is welcome to it."

"I appreciate it," Duncan said, popping open a can of beer and handing it over to Brooks before he sat back down on the cooler. "I hate to bust in on this bromance the two of you've got going. I know you don't get to town much these days, Lewis, with all your app inventions and technological leaps and bounds."

Brooks took a sip of beer and then pointed it at Lewis. "You don't know the half of it. He's got something so big in the works right now he's not even telling me about it."

"Not even telling your significant other, Lewis?" Vance Evans goaded. "That's harsh."

"Not as harsh as what the three of you pulled on Annabelle Devine," Lewis said through a laugh. "Explain to me again how a bogus three hundred dollar speeding ticket managed to get Duncan a date with the Keeper of the Debutantes."

"Yeah," Vance said, "because if three hundred dollars was all it took to snag a date with one of the Devine sisters, you would have worked that angle long ago."

"Damn straight," Lewis muttered before taking a swing of beer.

They were a sight, the four of them, Duncan surmised. Him sitting here in his casual business attire and expensive shoes. Vance and Brooks still in their uniforms, stretching their long, lanky, baseball-playing frames out in the beach chairs (clearly they'd done this a time or two)—and Lewis, the one who could buy and sell each of them a dozen times over wearing only a tattered t-shirt and jeans. Didn't anybody dress for the weather around here?

"What have the Devine sisters got against you, Lewis? I heard Annabelle say something about you this afternoon when she was all whipped-up into a frenzy."

"Yeah, what do they have against you?" Brooks teased. He and Vance bumped beer cans and laughed.

"Oh," Duncan apologized. "Sore subject, I see. Sorry I brought it up."

"No," Lewis held up his hand, nodding his head. "It's all right. I feel the wind of change coming, my boys, and tonight is going to be the night."

"The night for what, exactly?" Vance demanded.

"Tonight is the night I'm not only kissing Grace at midnight, I'm also going to tell her exactly how I feel."

The deafening silence that ensued declared Lewis' plan a bad idea.

"For ten years I've been the brunt of their game. And maybe I contributed to it all along," Lewis admitted.

"You think?" Brooks joked.

"But I'm twenty-nine now. I have my own company, a respectable degree of success, and it's time to make a stand. Those girls and I are too old for teenage games, and it's time Miss Gracie Devine put up or shut up. I'm going to make the woman mine...or die trying."

Unwilling to let the poor guy drown in silence again, Duncan spoke up. "Good for you, Lewis." Which encouraged Vance and Brooks to chime in with an "Absolutely" and an "Atta-boy."

"You know, Lewis," said Brooks, "there *are* other women. Other than the Devine sisters, I mean. While you're all manned-up and throwing your weight around tonight, take a look around you. You might have overlooked a pretty young thing you've been missing out on all these years."

"I've had eyes for Grace for so long, I can't even remember when I didn't."

"I hear you. But you and she don't even live in the same state anymore. And you see each other one time a year, at this party. What kind of relationship are you expecting?"

Lewis tossed his arms out in exasperation. "I just want the girl to kiss me, Brooks. Just one time, I want her to kiss me like she means it. That's my goal for the night. Been my goal all year now. If I manage to achieve that goal, I'll just have to figure out the rest."

Brooks nodded his head. "Fair enough."

"So," Duncan asked, in an effort to get Lewis off the hook as well as to satisfy his own curiosity, "tell me more about this Keeper of the Debutantes. Why do you call Annabelle that?"

"Oh, *we* don't just call her that," Vance said flinging his hand around to indicate the group.

"Everyone calls her that," Brooks added.

"It's who she is," Lewis explained. "You see, Annabelle has a lot of interests."

"Yeah, like ballroom dancing and etiquette classes," Vance said as he reached into a bag of Cheetos. "Which fork goes with what course—"

"Thank you notes and penmanship—"

"Proper attire, flowers, social teas, and charity events. She takes after her old Great-Aunt Helen in that regard."

Duncan swore he saw them all shudder at the mention of Great-Aunt Helen.

"Don't worry," Brooks said. "She's actually nothing like her great-aunt. She just appreciates all the old-school ways. Back when Tess made her debut in Raleigh, Annabelle—who is five years younger—took great interest and became an expert on what and who our Henderson debs needed to know. She coached the other debutantes from Henderson right along with Tess. And the powers that be in our little town—"

"Meaning the old biddies who give a rat's ass about that kind of stuff," Vance threw in.

"—asked Annabelle to help out the following year. Eventually, it was Annabelle who met with the debutantes' mothers and oversaw all the party-planning, gown-picking and whatever the hell else goes on with all that."

"She was good at it too," Lewis insisted. "I mean, we all clearly hated the re-establishment of cotillion classes. And since we were over the normal age of all that nonsense, they had special classes for us teens back then. But, the debutante parties went from stale to rip-roaring. It's amazing what kind of behavior you can get away with on the dance floor as long as your manners at the dinner table are impeccable."

"And you're dressed appropriately," Vance added.

"And you've flirted with a few of the wallflowers, along with their mothers, sisters and great-aunts," Brooks finished.

"We all learned something when the Keeper of the Debs was created," Lewis went on. "There is not a man in this town who doesn't know how to tie a bow tie, or dress for a five o'clock wedding. Annabelle upgraded the status of Henderson's social elite in the eyes of Raleigh's blue bloods, and at the same time the town became known for their swinging parties."

"Like the one you've wheedled your way into tonight." Brooks smiled at Duncan. "The Devine-Kampmueller New Year's Eve Ball is always kickin' ass and taking names."

"So all these years you all have been holding out on me."

Brooks leaned back and took a long swig of his beer. To Duncan it looked like he was hiding a laugh. "Timing is everything," Brooks finally said. "And I'm thinking the time's just about right."

~❧~

Those words rang inside Duncan's head when he got his first glimpse of Annabelle that night.

He stood in the cold, outside on the grand porch of Henderson

Country Club. He was purposely early. He thought it would be prudent to re-introduce himself to Annabelle without a large crowd around. Given that he was not, actually, Officer Friendly, or an officer at all—and that he'd given her a hard time and a three hundred dollar ticket this afternoon in order to win a bet—her reaction may not be in keeping with the impeccable manners she was known for.

And, feeling the tightness in his chest, he knew he deserved whatever penalty she dished out. He only hoped she didn't have him thrown out of the party before he could coax her into giving Duncan James, attorney at law, a chance.

He swore he saw snowflakes drifting around him as he stared through the side panel windows of the double front doors of the club. The round foyer appeared to be lit in gold, giving warmth to the scene before him. Annabelle Devine took his breath away. Literally. He stood motionless, not sure if he was conjuring up a character from Homer's *Odyssey*, because the gown Annabelle wore was straight out of Greek lore. Her silhouette displayed a graceful bare shoulder and arm and sheer flowing white fabric cascading to the ground. Her long red hair had been twisted up on her head in a sexy mess he hoped to get a chance to touch. Sooner rather than later.

There was a small crowd in front of Annabelle. Several younger women, all dressed in white ball gowns, stood in various stages of attention, but all were focused on what Annabelle was saying. She was animated, using her hands to direct her protégés. Behind them, proud parents stood, half listening, half talking amongst themselves. Eventually, the girls held their hands out for inspection. Given a nod, they pulled on their elbow-length gloves, except for one. After a brief discussion, Annabelle nodded and the one girl moved to hand her gloves to the coat check attendant behind Annabelle.

When she returned to the group, Annabelle gathered the girls tightly together and whispered for their ears only. To Duncan, it seemed like a football huddle, a secret game plan for the evening being discussed and agreed on. And then, in one happy moment, laughter erupted from all and the group disbanded, moving about in all directions.

Annabelle watched them go. Beaming, he noticed, like a proud momma. "The Keeper of the Debutantes," he whispered. He heard movement behind him and turned to find Brooks Bennett's parents coming up the porch steps.

"Mr. and Mrs. Bennett," Duncan addressed them, reaching out his hand in greeting.

Mr. Bennett took it and shook it sharply. "Well, I'll be. Duncan James. How are you, son?"

"I'm doing fine, Mr. Bennett. Thank you. Mrs. Bennett, you look lovely, as ever." He leaned in to kiss her cheek.

"Oh, I always love having you boys around." She tapped his cheek. "Are you here for the party?"

"I am.

"Well, good. You have a place to stay overnight? I don't want you driving back to Raleigh after drinking in here."

"I'm staying out at Brooks' place."

"In that mess?" Mrs. Bennett cried. "You come stay at our house."

"Well, thanks for the invitation, but don't you have Lewis staying there?"

"We do, but we have plenty of room. In fact, I don't know why Brooks insists on staying at his place while it's under construction. He could move right back into his old room and at least be comfortable while he's fixin' that place up."

Duncan smiled at being given the perfect opportunity to set Brooks up. "Sounds like the smart plan to me. I don't know what he's thinking."

"Exactly. So we'll see you both later tonight."

"Come on, woman," Mr. Bennett said, placing a hand under her arm and steering her toward the door. He looked back at Duncan and winked. "If we miss you tonight, be sure to stop by for our Rose Bowl party tomorrow."

"I'm looking forward to it."

He stood another moment before following the Bennetts through the door. It was eight o'clock and cars were starting to stream into the circular drive. If Duncan didn't want a crowd when he first spoke to Annabelle, he'd better git-r-done.

CHAPTER FOUR

Annabelle's breath caught as soon as she spied Duncan coming through the doors. She recognized his luxurious coat and Ryan Seacrest hairstyle. His face was still a bit of a mystery since he'd been wearing those clichéd mirrored cop shades this afternoon. She had the urge to pat her hair and wet her lips just glimpsing his profile. Instead, she took a deep breath to steady herself as John and Ellen Bennett came forward to greet her.

"Annabelle, wait until you see our Darcy this evening," Mrs. Bennett said as she beamed proudly. "I swear since she's moved to Boston her inner debutante has revealed itself. She's transformed, I tell you. She started with LASIK surgery and is ending with a designer ball gown. Trust me, you will not believe your eyes."

"Hardly recognized my own daughter," Mr. Bennett added.

"Well, that is something," Annabelle agreed. "Darcy dragged her feet through the entire debutante shopping experience. I wonder what has caused the change."

Out of the corner of her eye, Annabelle watched Duncan hang back as the three of them talked. She also noticed his slight grimace when he was brought to her attention by Mrs. Bennett.

"Annabelle, dear. Have you been introduced to Duncan James?" Mrs. Bennett motioned for him to come join them. "We've known him quite a while now and we're very proud of him. He's with a law practice in Raleigh. You live in Raleigh too, don't you?"

Game on.

"I do live in Raleigh," Annabelle agreed. "But I'm afraid you're mistaken, Mrs. Bennett. This man is a special agent brought in to work with Henderson's finest. In fact, I believe he was riding with Brooks today."

John Bennett uttered an "Uh-oh," while glancing over at Duncan.

"Well, no, I don't think so," his wife said, confused.

"Yes," Annabelle insisted, turning her attention from Mrs. Bennett to Duncan. "I'm sure this is the officer who gave me a speeding ticket this afternoon. Isn't that right?"

Annabelle felt sorry for Brooks' father. The man immediately started to shift from one foot to the other, grabbing for the coat at his wife's shoulders, trying to turn her attention away from the conversation. "Ellen, sweetheart, let me help you with your coat."

"Well, no, Anna—*John!* What are you doing?"

Annabelle met Duncan's eyes over the Bennetts' tussle. He stood tall, his weight evenly distributed. His hands were clasped behind him making no effort to hide the telltale cashmere coat he had worn that afternoon. The same one, in fact, he had so gallantly wrapped around her. His eyes were yellow-gold and met her gaze full-on, unashamed and resolved to face whatever wrath she chose to dish out.

Brave. She liked that.

"Officer Friendly," she said, tipping her head to the right indicating they should take a couple of steps away to have a more private conversation. He followed her lead.

"Duncan James," he said, his eyes recapturing her gaze and holding it as she offered her hand at his introduction. Her father was right. He did have a firm handshake and solid eye contact.

"Annabelle Devine."

"Keeper of the Debutantes."

"You know about that?" She ducked her chin thinking the title had worn off. At the same time, she felt his thumb move back and forth over her hand. She kinda liked that.

"I know a little. I'm hoping you'll tell me more."

It was how he offered a sort-of apology, combining it with a declaration of interest all put out there with the smoking rich timbre of his voice that had Annabelle feeling lightheaded. She licked her lips, gathering her thoughts.

"And Mrs. Bennett said you're a lawyer. Prosecution or defense?"

"Neither. Corporate attorney."

What a shame for women on juries everywhere, she thought.

He cleared his throat. "Annabelle, I hope you'll forgive me for that little…ah, prank, this afternoon."

"Was I not speeding?"

His body shot to attention, fire amplifying the gold in his eyes. "Hell yes, you were speeding. You and that rocket ship were in ludicrous-speed when you roared by."

"So, I deserved a ticket."

"You did. Without doubt."

"But you're feeling guilty because my three hundred dollars isn't going to *help out* the city of Henderson as you suggested, but *is* going to settle the bet you won with Brooks and Vance."

Duncan moved his head around and adjusted his shoulders. "Ah, apparently someone has sold me out."

"Indeed. But before you go and lose your Man Card by offering my money back, let me tell you that I consider that payment for our date tonight. And as I remember, you—well, you in your Officer Friendly persona—promised me 'as much service as I can handle.'"

The color of his cheeks heightened. Trapped in so many ways Duncan opened and closed his mouth but none of that rich, sexy lawyer talk was forthcoming. She smiled broadly, satisfied to wait as he continued to try to conjure a response.

"I…I simply do not know what to say to all that," he started. "I mean…Man Card? Really? Payment for our date? And…what was that? As much *service* as you can handle? Annabelle," he said shaking his head, "if someone overheard you, your position as Queen Bee of the Debutantes would be revoked."

"It's Keeper of the Debutantes," she corrected.

"That, too. And Brooks and Vance would have to haul both our asses in. Me for soliciting and you for buying."

"Oh," she said sweetly, "let's not use ugly words like solicitation."

"That's what it is."

"I know, but let's just not call it that."

Duncan pressed his lips into a firm line, saying absolutely

nothing. But Annabelle felt the scolding heat of his you're-pushing-it stare slowly penetrate all seven layers of her skin.

Hot, hot, hot. *Seriously* sexy.

And then...then he started unbuttoning his coat. Slowly. Deliberately. Annabelle grew flushed, becoming keenly aware of a smoldering longing flaring up as she watched him disrobe.

He pulled off his coat and carefully folded it over one arm. Then, in his quietest baritone, he said, "I swear to God, if you lick those lips one more time, I'm going to pull you obscenely close and kiss you long and hard right here by the front door."

Her mouth parted in awe. "Was I really licking my lips?" she whispered.

He gave one short nod.

"Well, you can hardly blame me," she said, pointing her finger up and down his body. "Wow."

Duncan James, with his stylishly tossed dark head of hair and angular features softened only by the dimple in his chin, stood one head taller than her five-foot-seven-in-heels frame. He wore a tuxedo that was well-tailored to his broad shoulders and narrow hips. From head to pricey shoes, his style was classic. Impeccable. He knew what looked good on him and he knew how to wear it. She could have wept for the perfection standing before her. Instead, she stopped herself just as she was about to lick her lips.

"Good girl," he said. "Now, let me get rid of my coat and we can move this date to a quieter location."

For a moment she thought he meant they would leave the party, and it surprised her that she would have gladly followed him right out the door. Not the best form for a hostess. Even though the invitation was officially sent by their parents, Tess, Grace and Annabelle did their part to make the evening the smashing success it was year after year. But, as Annabelle watched the throng of regulars arrive greeting one another with a "Happy New Year," she decided her usual duties as greeter could be forgone this year.

She turned as Duncan approached and offered his arm. She sighed at the gesture, smiling her approval and then pointed the way up the foyer steps. Besides—she thought, while taking his arm—someone really should make sure our newest guest has a very good time.

CHAPTER FIVE

When Annabelle snuggled her left hand under his upper arm and grabbed his bicep, Duncan felt a shot of adrenaline rush right to those muscles. Like he was Clark Kent transforming into Superman. And when she snuggled her entire body up against his side—so she could top her left hand with her right—he felt the soft mound of breast press against the side of his arm. His brain immediately pictured what she might look like naked from the waist up. As if he'd pulled out his ever-present Swiss army knife and in one cut had the fabric across her shoulder tumbling down, exposing her torso all the way to her hips. If the whole licking-her-lips porn scenario hadn't drained his brain of public decency, what little he had left was now heading south of his waistband, fast.

As they moved together on the staircase and up and out of the now-crowded foyer, his baser instincts had his nose turning toward her profile and drawing in the scent of roses that wafted off her throat. It was all he could do to not press his lips to the intriguing indentation where pale and slender neck met fit and shapely shoulder. He was even starting to relish the beginning sensations of his hard-on when one dreaded word burst from Annabelle's lips.

"Daddy!"

Talk about a cock block.

"Daddy, Mother," Annabelle called while maneuvering him a quarter of the way down a long, wide hallway lined with couches, tables and chairs. Out of the relative quiet, jarring music erupted from the ballroom to his right, and then—as if Duncan's nervous system hadn't been shocked enough in the last few milliseconds—his source of heat dropped her hands from around his bicep, leaving him internally shaken.

Public place. Parents around. And you don't even know this girl, Duncan's brain scolded as he held out his hand in response to the introductions going on around him. Get your damn head on straight, he thought even as he greeted Harry Devine. "That's correct, sir. Brooks Bennett introduced us back in early November. I think we were all here watching the State-Carolina football game."

"That's exactly right," Mr. Devine said. "I remember you and your boys surrounded by a few shot glasses and a pitcher of beer. Can't blame you. That Wolfpack of yours took a damn beating that day."

Duncan laughed. "That they did, sir. That they did."

"This is my wife, Jody." Harry beamed with pride as he introduced Annabelle's mother. Other than the hair and eye color, there was a very strong family resemblance between mother and daughter. No wonder the man beamed.

"A beautiful party, Mrs. Devine," Duncan said as he took her extended hand.

"Why, thank you, Duncan. We're happy you could join us." He didn't miss the meaningful look Jody Devine gave her daughter.

"And here comes our precious Grace," Harry went on. "Gracie-girl! Darling," he called, motioning a fairy-princess to join their group.

The epitome of Cinderella-at-the-ball started their way, lean and graceful—until she settled directly between Duncan and Annabelle hoisting the strapless ball gown up under her armpits and fixing her bosoms to sit a little perkier under the gossamer fabric.

Duncan had to bite the inside of his cheek not to laugh at Annabelle's horrified expression. "My God, Grace. If you touch the bodice of that gown one more time I'm going to rip it off you. I swear it!"

"I thought it was falling down, Belly. What? You want me running around exposing myself all night?"

"Belly?" Duncan asked.

"I've told you over and over, the dress can't fall," Annabelle insisted. "Pretend it's like your gun holster. *You* wear the dress. Stop letting the dress wear you."

Grace leaned her head to the side, considering. "Huh. Okay, I get it now." She turned to her sister. "Done. And thank you."

Annabelle just nodded in satisfaction.

Mr. Devine picked up the introductions. "Duncan James, my second daughter, Gracie-belle."

"Grace," she insisted, holding her hand out to Duncan. "Just Grace. No belle."

"Got it," Duncan nodded.

"So you're the hero who gave my sister her first speeding ticket," she said, still holding his hand.

Duncan felt another shot of adrenaline, this one heating up his face. His gaze bounced around the members of the Devine family gathered before him, not sure where that prank placed him in their estimation. "I cannot tell a lie," he offered. "I was the one who gave Annabelle the ticket."

"Good for you," Grace said. "About damn time. And what did you think of that car she was driving? Too damn loud. Way too fast. The term *redneck* comes to mind every time I see the damn thing."

"Gracie-belle," her father broke in. "Do I need to remind you we are at a party, not one of your field interrogations? Your language, peanut."

"She does have a broader vocabulary than she's letting on," Jody Devine assured him.

"Sorry," Grace offered. "But that car of hers just makes me crazy. It's absurd for Belly to be riding around in that thing. She's going to kill herself."

"I like the car," Duncan confessed with a quick wink to Annabelle. "Call me a redneck, but I'm trying to figure out what I need to do to be able to test-drive that machine."

Harry laughed as Grace groaned. Annabelle stepped in between Duncan and Grace, securing his bicep in her left hand again. "Well, I don't know about a test drive, Mr. James. But that comment certainly gets you a free drink at the bar," she said, turning him away from the ballroom and her family, toward the open doors on the other side of the hall. "We'll see ya'll a bit later on," she said in parting.

"Stop on by the house tomorrow," her father said to Duncan as they headed off. "We'll talk more football during the Rose Bowl."

"Will do, Mr. Devine. Thanks." Duncan let Annabelle lead him away. He didn't know why she and her family were letting him get away with impersonating an officer so easily, but the fact that they had lulled him into a wonderful sense of security.

Met the parents. Check. Met the tough, gun-toting sister. Check. The night had hardly begun and Duncan felt buoyant having managed his perceived mine field so quickly and easily. His ego was puffed up and in full riot gear when Annabelle stopped him far short of the two very secluded seats he was spying at the far end of the bar. "And this is my sister, Tess," she announced.

Tess.

Beautiful. Vibrant. Sultry, bedroom-eyed Tess.

Who was also, very obviously—if not to Annabelle, then at least to himself—pissed off at the world, Tess.

The daggers her chocolate brown eyes shot at Duncan ripped his riot gear apart and had his ego lying at her tiny, little high-heeled feet.

Seated on a tall chair at the center of the bar and draped in wine red, Tess' lush and curvaceous body was turned sideways, her slender arm dangling over the back of the chair. A large cuff of sparkling diamonds circled her wrist as she pointed directly at his heart. He wasn't certain daggers weren't going to shoot from her fingertip as well.

"Dun-can Jaaames," she sung at him. "Man among men! Infamous," she pronounced. "Tell me, Duncan James, with your GQ hair-style and your thousand-dollar tuxedo," she said, swirling her pointed finger all around him. "How is it, exactly," she said as her eyes narrowed, "that you are able to give my baby sister an outrageous speeding ticket in the afternoon, and then dare to have your hands all over her at our father's party tonight?"

So much for not stepping on a fucking land mine.

"Don't mind, Tess," Annabelle said turning toward him with a light-hearted smile. "She has a wonderful sense for the dramatic. Which serves her really well in all her roles on Broadway. Doesn't it, Tess?"

Tess threw Annabelle a sarcastic grin.

"Since she's the one Devine sister without a date tonight, it appears she's taking her frustration out on you. I'm guessing she's been imagining Lewis Kampmueller's hands all over her during their kiss at midnight. Am I right?"

Tess turned back to the bar and lifted her drink. "At least we know he's a good kisser," she said before taking a gulp. "Who knows about Officer Friendly there."

Duncan slipped his arm around Annabelle's waist and looked down into her pretty brown eyes. "She's got you there." Then he lifted his attention to the back of Tess' head. "His bank statement beats the hell out of mine as well, but I guess you Devine sisters aren't worried about all that. However...." He took a step toward Tess, bringing Annabelle with him so he could whisper in Tess' ear. "It's my understanding that the highly respected Mr. Kampmueller is interested in only one of the Devine sisters tonight. Forgive me for saying this, *Tess*, but you're not the one he's picturing getting his hands on at midnight."

Tess turned her head sideways and gave him her first honest smile. "Grace has always been the one he thinks he's in love with," she said kindly, showing her true feelings about Lewis. "And if Annabelle and I have our way again this year, he'll be kissing the one he wants come midnight. Michael-schmichael."

"Grace's date," Annabelle explained.

"Ah. A stumbling block for Lewis."

"Perhaps," Tess said. "We'll have to see how it all works out." Then she waved them away, a queen dismissing her court.

With a hand on the small of her back, Duncan directed Annabelle to the farthest two bar chairs tucked close to the back wall of the room. "Your father seems awfully relaxed for a man who has three gorgeous daughters," he said.

"That's sweet of you to say," Annabelle responded as he helped her into the last chair. It was an intentional move. Duncan hoped that his body would block her from view for a while. He was as social as the next guy, but having survived the last half hour, he needed a breather before encountering any more family or friends. Besides, he thought as he took a serious look at the elegance settling herself beside him, he needed all the time he could get to make a lasting impression on this particularly beautiful Devine sister. He wanted a second date on the books by the end of the night.

"So what's your drink, Annabelle?"

"Bourbon and Ginger Ale."

"Is that right? A true Southern belle."

"Uh-huh. And how 'bout yourself?"

"Beer, generally," he said. But when the bartender stepped toward them he ordered, "Two tequila shots."

The young, dark-headed bartender stopped dead in his tracks. From the expression on his face he was obviously trying to figure something out. "You want them with the cut-up limes and a shaker of salt?"

"That'd be good," Duncan nodded. "First night on the job?"

A magical smile lit up the young man's face. "Something like that," he said. "Two shots, coming right up."

"Tequila shots?" Annabelle threw Duncan a sideways glance.

"Hey. Midnight rolls around and I'm lucky enough to be kissing you, I want you just tipsy enough that you aren't comparing me to Lewis Kampmueller."

Annabelle burst out laughing. "Are you actually worried about outshining Lewis in the kissing department?"

Hell yes! "No."

Annabelle leaned her shoulder over and nudged him in the arm. "Really?"

He wobbled his head from side to side, causing her to grin. At least it looked like a grin from his peripheral vision. At the moment, he found himself unable to face her. What if he didn't kiss better than Lewis?

Jesus, he cursed at himself. *Man up, dude.*

As the bartender arranged the shots in front of them, Annabelle noticed his name tag. "Your name's Harry?"

"That's right," he said, wiping his hands on the towel tucked into his waistband. He held out his hand to Annabelle and the cuff of his white shirt pulled up. Duncan noticed a tattoo on his wrist. It looked like a quiver holding six arrows.

"Harry," she nodded, taking his hand and shaking it. "That's a good name. My father's name in fact."

"Is that right?"

She nodded. "Harry, would you bring another round of shots when you have a chance? Sounds like Mr. James needs help with his performance anxiety."

Duncan slapped his hand on the bar, turned his head and laid a disbelieving stare on Annabelle. He could hear the mirth Bartender Harry tried to smother as he headed off to do her bidding, but he didn't take his eyes from the one he wanted now more than ever. God, he could never have conjured up all the perfect pieces that made up this woman. The same thought he'd had hours before rang out clearly in his mind.

I have found you.

He had. He knew it. And maybe, just maybe, Annabelle Devine knew it too. Because without a doubt, she had just thrown down the gauntlet…and he was more than willing to pick it up.

Duncan nodded his chin at the set of shot glasses. "Let's see who has performance anxiety."

Annabelle's eyes sparkled as she turned her attention to the tequila. Duncan followed just a split second behind as they licked the skin between their finger and thumb, poured on the salt, licked it clean, downed the shot, and then bit into the wedge of lime. He was certain the grimace on her face was far worse than his own.

He wiped his lips with the back of a hand while The Keeper dabbed hers with a cocktail napkin. It reminded him of something. "Pretty impressive. Where did you develop your expertise?"

"Tequila Shoot-Out. Zate House. Fall semester, sophomore year."

"Ah." Duncan nodded knowingly. "Wild night?"

"Can't say for sure. But nothing ended up on Facebook, so except for the insane hangover the next day, I think I made it through relatively unscathed."

"Miss Manners. At a tequila shoot-out." He tried to imagine Annabelle the debutante coed.

"But you're more than a book on manners, you know. You are gracious."

"Thank you. Isn't that one and the same?"

"Not at all," he stalled while Bartender Harry and his quiver full of arrows set up a second round. "For instance," he went on quietly as the bartender moved away, "our young friend here offered his hand to you. You know that a book of etiquette says a gentleman never offers his hand to a lady, but waits to have her hand offered to him," he said drawing on his own cotillion experience. "And yet you don't stand on principal. You shook his hand without pause."

"Well, of course. Otherwise it would have created a terribly awkward moment."

"Exactly my point. You were gracious. You *are* gracious."

She fed him a brilliant smile, and leaned in closer. "And you are going to get a hell of a kiss come midnight."

Oh, I'll be getting more than a kiss, he promised himself, glancing at his watch discreetly. Maybe the tequila had already started talking. More likely it was Annabelle's easy humor and the way his body simmered in a state of rapt attention wherever she touched him. And, he noted, she was touching him a lot. But most likely, it was the mounting anticipation of getting his hands on the bare flesh of all those curves covered in just the sheerest of fabrics—so sheer he swore he saw the dark coloration of the tips of her beasts when he dared allow his glance to go there. In his mind, she wore nothing underneath that dress, and he was starting to get just a little desperate to find out if he was right. To hell with a damn kiss at midnight. He wanted some time alone with Miss Devine and he wanted it as soon as he could get it.

CHAPTER SIX

The bar area with its masculine wood architecture and hunter green accents had filled up nicely, and the conversations which ensued created a lovely warm hum that had Annabelle sinking cozily into their little twosome at the far end of the bar. Her body was now turned sideways in her seat, her back literally against the wall. Duncan's frame had likewise turned towards her, and his broad shoulders and taller height blocked her vision of any guest coming or going. It was perfect.

It was perfect how her knees fit between his and how his inner thighs would brush against her outer thighs as the two of them conversed with an extraordinary amount of animation. It was perfect how his arm laid along the back of her chair, and his fingers would stroke her bare skin from time to time. His touch created the perfect little goosebumps on the outside of her skin and the perfect blast of heat that ran itself ragged on the inside. But the most perfect thing of all was the moment right after their second shot, when they laughed and caught each other's happy gaze. The world around them stopped, going quiet. That moment…that perfect moment…when their lips were only inches apart and her heartbeat pounded in her ears, when Duncan laced his fingers with hers and brought her hand up, turning it slowly, and placed a kiss on the sensitive skin of the inside of her wrist.

It was romantic and subtle and stole her heart. And it was then that Annabelle realized she had better get to know a little more about her Officer Friendly if she was going to go home and announce to her sisters that she planned to marry Duncan James.

"So growing up in Richmond, you decided to go to NC State?"

"I didn't have the grades to get into Chapel Hill. I figured it was the next best thing. And don't laugh, Little Miss North Carolina. In the end, it truly was the right place for me. I met Brooks and Vance and we formed a close-knit group, bonding over our college experience. We shared a lot of good times. But more than that, they always had my back. And they still do today. Best thing that ever happened to me."

Annabelle loved the way he spoke about his friends and their solid relationship. "But you went to UNC for law school?"

"Well," Duncan said, eyeing her over a sip of water, "I'm stupid but I ain't crazy." She laughed. "I set my sights on law school at Carolina before I set foot on campus at NC State. I like the south, and staying in North Carolina kept me closer to home. So, my goal was to get straight A's because I was not going to be turned down again."

"And you got them."

"I got them," he acknowledged.

"So are you a hard worker or are you just that smart?"

"Well, now." He leaned in close, his light Southern accent noticeably heavier. "I'm sitting here with you, aren't I?"

Annabelle bit her lip, trying not to show the pleasure that his answer gave her. "Well, unless you majored in drama, I'd say playing the part of Officer Friendly today was pretty hard work."

"But gettin' you to insist I be your escort tonight…now that was brilliant." He flashed an arrogant grin before adding, "And thanks for goin' easy on me about all that, by the way."

A pang of guilt about what had really gone down threatened to intrude, but Annabelle shoved it away. Things were going too well to jeopardize the evening with a confession. "Am I detecting a slightly heavier Southern drawl?"

Duncan sat back with his arms crossed over his chest, grinning broadly. With each word he sat up a little straighter and moved in a little closer. "I'm pretty certain that a couple of tequila shots and a pretty Southern belle could reduce me to sounding a lot more like Redneck One and Redneck Two than usual."

"Brooks and Vance?"

"You catch on quick."

"Those two are sort of celebrities around here."

"And don't I know it. They took State to three College World Series. Won one of them on a no-hitter from Brooks. Man, those guys could play."

"So how is it you knew you wanted to go to law school before you even started college?"

"No choice in that." Duncan shrugged. "I was born to it. My dad is a criminal defense attorney, and if that's not bad enough, my mother is a judge."

"Your mother is a judge?" Annabelle exclaimed wide-eyed.

"That's right. And we aren't talking Judge Judy, although at home she settled our disagreements about the same way, I suppose."

"You have brothers and sisters?" Annabelle asked, finding all of this fascinating.

"Three sisters and one brother. I'm the oldest. Then the girls—Molly, Lacey and Abigail. Then Jesse."

"Your brother's name is Jesse James?" When Duncan nodded, Annabelle laughed so hard she snorted.

"Oh my God, that's the first unladylike thing I've seen you do," Duncan said, grinning from ear to ear. "You are a mere mortal after all, aren't you?"

"I am indeed," she agreed. "Seriously, Jesse James?"

"My parents might be lawyers, but they are lawyers with a sense of humor. And they probably needed a good reminder of that when kid number five arrived."

"Annabelle!" A deep-pitched baritone from the other end of the bar caused Duncan to turn. Annabelle probably wouldn't have noticed it—so enthralled with the man in front of her—but following Duncan's lead, she looked down the bar as tall, blond and long-ago heartthrob, Stubs McKenna started to call her name again.

"Anna— Oh, there you are," Stubs said as he spied her down the way. He pointed his finger at her and started muscling his way through the crowd gathered at the bar to get to them.

Duncan's disgruntled protest gave her great satisfaction as she assured him this would only take a minute. With eyes only for

Annabelle, Stubs landed a heavy hand on Duncan's shoulder, only acknowledging him with a quick "Hey, Bud," before shoving his head in the space between Duncan and herself to plant a big ol' kiss on her cheek. Annabelle was pretty sure she saw her date stiffen. Another boost to her feminine pride. "Come on now," Stubs said, holding out his hand, "the band is kicking serious ass. Why are you crammed back here in the corner? You know you're my go-to gal on the dance floor."

Duncan, whose arms were crossed over his chest, glanced down at Stub's big hand sitting on his shoulder, then up into Stubs' face as he blurted all this out. Then he rolled his eyes dramatically toward Annabelle, giving her a direct look that said, "You have got to be kidding me."

She winked and held up one finger to Duncan, seeking a little patience. "Well, bless your heart, Stubs," she started, turning her full attention to the man. "How thoughtful of you to come find me when there are so many other pretty girls just dying for you to ask them to dance. In fact," she went on, turning Stubs' attention where she wanted it, "Katherine Stuart was asking about you the moment she arrived. See her over there, just out in the hallway?" She gave him a little push in the right direction. "Now you be the gentleman and go on and give that girl a thrill."

Annabelle and Duncan watched as Stubs ambled away. "Well, I'll be," Duncan whispered, then turned his attention back to Annabelle. "It was like you put that lummox in a trance and he didn't have the capability not to follow your orders."

She took a sip of water. "Oh, he's just a big ol' sweetheart. Probably didn't even realize he was intruding. Now, where were we?"

Duncan took her hand in his and bounced it up and down. "You know, I was thinking," he said, "you were probably an undergraduate while I was in law school at Carolina. We were on the same campus. I wonder if our paths ever crossed."

"I highly doubt it," Annabelle scoffed. "Sounds like you were probably in the law library, and I have to admit, I was rarely in any library at all. I did not go to college to make the dean's list, much to my parents' chagrin."

"Is that so?" Duncan's expression was priceless. A combination of amusement and wonder.

"Well, of course I wanted a good education, and I got it. My only redeeming academic achievement is that I never ever missed a class. Which I repeatedly pointed out to my father whenever he started ranting and raving about my grades and the cost of tuition. I assured him I was getting his money's worth, and I did. More than most students, because I filled every hour with a group or club. There were just too many enticing activities and too much stuff to learn to justify spending more than the minimal amount of time necessary studying for tests."

"Is that a fact? So what sorts of things, pray tell, enticed the youngest Devine sister?"

"Basketball. I wanted to make sure I got inside the Dean Dome for every home game, so I finagled a job babysitting the VIP alumni. You know, show them to their seats, make sure they have everything they could want, schmooze them into bigger donations." She flashed him a cheeky smile. "I was good at that."

"I don't doubt it."

"Then, of course, the sorority. Which has become my career. I'm our acting Field Representative for all the Atlantic Coast colleges, keeping all the garish behavior of uninspired coeds out of the public's eye. I've become very good at putting out fires," she smirked.

"And inspiring better behavior?"

"They don't call me Keeper of the Debutantes for nothing. But back in college I served as Rush Chairman, was our Panhellenic Delegate junior year and then was the Philanthropy Chair. Other than that...." She sighed, thinking, counting the rest out on her fingers as she spoke, "I participated in the Synchronized Swim Club, the French Club, the Auto Mechanics Club, and then all the usual. You know, Habitat for Humanity, Big Sisters of Durham, and Santa Claus Anonymous."

Duncan stared at her blankly. "Is my head actually spinning? Because who the hell knew there was synchronized swimming and I just can't picture you in the Auto Mechanics Club to save my life!"

"And yet, you've seen the car I drive."

"Good point."

Archibald Reynolds jostled his way up to them, looking like

he'd been on a roll shaking hands and kissing babies all night. "Hey there, Buddy," he said taking Duncan's hand and shaking it. "How you doin'?" The expression suited whether he was supposed to know the person he was addressing or not. Duncan didn't appear to be amused. Especially when Archie turned his back on Duncan, essentially blocking him from Annabelle. "Now you know, sugar, if you sit in this corner all night your momma's party is just gonna roll over and play dead. Sweetheart, you need to come with me and be seen on the dance floor. Now don't try and tell me no."

Noticing Duncan's hand landing on Archie's shoulder, Annabelle gestured. "May I introduce my date," she said quickly as Duncan spun Archie around. "Archie, this is Duncan James. He's a good friend of Brooks Bennett and Vance Evans. Duncan, this is Archibald Reynolds, a family friend."

Duncan eyed Archie as the other man's whiskey came dangerously close to sloshing over the rim of his glass. "Brooks, you say? Well, any friend of Brooks...." He turned back to Annabelle. "Find me later on, honey, and I'll give you a twirl." With that, he downed the last of his bourbon, toasted the couple with his empty glass and brought it down heavily on the bar in between them. He scooped his long blond bangs out of his face before turning and dissolving into the crowd.

"Give you a twirl?" Duncan squinted. "What the hell does that mean?"

"I'm sure he meant a twirl on the dance floor."

"Yeah. Right." After holding her gaze, Duncan rubbed his jaw, glancing around the room. "I have to give you credit, Annabelle Devine. You sure know how to handle the awkward social situation."

"Well, as the expression goes, 'This ain't my first rodeo'."

"Ha," Duncan let out a short laugh. "I bet. Seems about time to order up a real drink. Bourbon and Ginger?"

"That'd be perfect," Annabelle said, realizing how utterly tempting he looked now that the polished sheen had worn off. His hair was a little tousled and the color in his cheeks had risen. He'd unbuttoned his jacket and didn't look disheveled as much as loose. Or, was that his body spoiling for a fight? A tiny thrill rent its way through her, from front to back. Her breath hitched thinking about his annoyance at the interruptions. Dear Lord, there was something about this combination of impeccable manners and male aggression that had her softening into very malleable putty, longing to be in his hands.

Heaven help her, she was getting turned on just thinking about it.

When Harry the magical bartender delivered their drinks, Duncan handed him a tip and then lifted Annabelle's glass to her. As she sipped, he seemed to be trying to figure out something. Finally he tilted his bottled beer, took a swig, and then pointed it at her.

"You've given me something to think about, Annabelle. Something to look at differently than I have ever before."

"Really? What's that?"

"Something you said about your college experience. The way you looked at it. See," he said, glancing around the crowded room again before resting his gaze back on her. "I joined the Phi Deltas for a lot of reasons, but one of them truly was their motto: 'Become the greatest version of yourself.' To me, it seemed, I had already embraced that. Get the straight A's. Leave no question about getting into law school. Throw in civility, loyalty, respect for women and elders, that kind of thing, done. But you," he said, pointing the tip of his bottle toward her again, "you went and explored everything you could get your hands on. You…" he said thoughtfully, "you didn't let grades get in the way of your education. There!" he congratulated himself. "That's it."

"I had no use for grades because I wasn't going to law school. Or med school. Or any sort of graduate school. So, I had the luxury."

"Indeed. And now you can, what? Speak French?"

"Mais, oui!"

"And build a car from the ground up?"

"Maybe…with the proper tools."

He spread his arms wide. "And you're funny and clever and not only Keeper of the Debutantes, but the sorority girls as well. And," he said, "apparently you are a hell of a dancer because it seems everybody and their brother wants to give you a twirl."

"Oh, no."

"Oh, yes."

"No, I mean…oh, crap."

It was all the warning she could give before another hand landed hard on his shoulder, and another good ol' boy called him Buddy.

"Hey, Bud-dy!" Tucker Davenport put a big ee sound on the end of his greeting and Annabelle wasn't sure if that was what set Duncan off or whether it was the fact that he'd been knocked so hard his beer splashed out of the bottle. "Annabelle," Tucker said as he circled her wrist with his hand pulling her off her chair, "you've played wallflower long enough and it's time to come—"

Tucker stopped short when a large hand landed flat, hard and square in the center of his chest. He looked down at the hand, and then at the man attached to it.

"Release. My. Date."

Annabelle had never heard three words promise more. She actually had to choke back a laugh at the expression on Tucker's face. Tucker, who had a good fifty pounds on Duncan, looked as if a gun was being held to his head. In fact, after he released her wrist, he held both hands up and backed away.

Duncan said nothing more. The incident seemed to go unnoticed by anyone except the three of them. They both eyed Tucker until he finally turned and picked his way through the room and out the door. Hearing his long release of breath, Annabelle glanced up at Duncan.

"Are you okay?" he asked.

"Never. Been. Better," she said slowly and honestly, looking him straight in the eye. It was the best she could do to convey that he'd just handed her one of the biggest thrills of her life.

If his smile was any indication, he understood. "Really?"

"Really."

"Well then," he breathed, taking her by the hand. "Let's take these drinks and head on over to the dance floor. Maybe that will keep the goddamn vultures at bay."

CHAPTER SEVEN

It didn't escape Duncan's notice that Annabelle had to bite her lips to keep from smiling too big. Well, good, he thought as he led her through the bar. The last thing he wanted to do was embarrass her or himself. But he'd be damned if he was going to step aside tonight. Not for one minute was he willing to give up his time with Annabelle. He certainly hadn't intended to go all Neanderthal on her father's guests, but he was not about to step the fuck aside. Not now. Not ever.

He was rolling with a good head of steam when he saw them. Probably had every thought showing on his face too when, just across the hallway and standing at the entrance of the ballroom, Duncan spied the two biggest assholes on the face of the Earth. Son of a bitch, he thought, as Vance and Brooks burst out laughing the moment they saw him.

"You two," Duncan pointed. "Later," he promised.

"Why are they laughing?" Annabelle asked as they entered the ballroom. "You don't think they set all that up, do you?"

"I'm certain of it," Duncan said, raising his voice to be heard above the band. He continued to hold Annabelle's hand as he turned to face her. Behind her, the room was rocking. The large ballroom was jammed with party-goers, most of whom were dancing—and, from the looks of all the discarded jackets, sweating as well. Beyond that mayhem, the band put on a show. With a brass section and backup dancers, no wonder everyone wanted to be on the dance floor. "Man, this is some party," he said over her head.

"Why would they do that?"

Duncan looked into Annabelle's upturned face and couldn't help but smile. She was indignant on his behalf. Almost made it all worth it. He carefully took the glass out of her hand and held up a finger indicating she should wait there. He stashed their drinks on a side table littered with purses, cocktail napkins, half-finished drinks and even ladies' shoes. When he came back, he slid an arm around her waist and pulled her in close to speak against her ear.

"Brooks and Vance think I don't like to dance."

Annabelle pulled back and looked up at him with a cautious expression. He tugged her back to him intending to say more. But her heat and her scent had every neuron in his brain zeroing in on the soft, pale skin just below his lips. As if in a trance, he closed his eyes and leaned in to bite the tender spot between her neck and shoulder. Abruptly, he caught himself, his body immediately pumping adrenaline at the misstep. *Jesus H. Christ. Sweet Mother Mary.* He felt his heart pounding against his ribcage. His brain had shut down and his libido had gone commando. *I am a complete goner.* He swallowed before he could remember what he'd intended to say. When words came out they were thick, and full of want. "What Brooks and Vance don't know is, I actually *do* like to dance. It just has to be with the *right partner.*"

Almost afraid to look at her, Duncan unwrapped himself and started to back up, slowly pulling Annabelle onto the dance floor. When his eyes finally made their way to her face, he was richly rewarded by the soft, tender expression waiting for him. Well, dang. Apparently he did have a way with words.

Duncan acknowledged that a lot of things had to be in alignment for him to have a good time on any dance floor. Two shots of tequila and a beer didn't hurt. A kick-ass band could get him most of the way there. But he'd told the truth—having the right partner was key. Because while his attention was on Annabelle, thoughts of looking like an idiot out here didn't bother to intrude.

While dancing over the course of the set, one of the things Duncan found wildly entertaining was watching Annabelle and her sisters dance around each other. They had this habit of hiking their gowns clear up to the tops of their thighs—and we're talking some sweet-looking thighs. He expected Mrs. Devine to run out and swat all those dresses down at some point, but then he saw the darnedest thing. Mrs. Devine came running all right. But they must have been playing the family theme song because all the girls gathered where he and Annabelle were dancing, and even Mrs. Devine had the hem of her dress swishing around some very shapely thighs. Huh. It wasn't quite ten o'clock and the Keeper and her mother were flashing the crowd. Damned if Brooks wasn't right. This New Year's Eve ball was kickin' ass and taking names.

And as much fun as all that was, the elation he felt when a slow song began to play could have raised the Titanic. Because there was nothing he wanted to do more than get his hands on the ball of fire in front of him.

However, he was not going to swing her into his arms like an eager teen. No. He was of a mind to savor this coming together. Savor the first time he'd take this fast-drivin', law-breakin', debutante-makin', quick-witted beauty into his arms. So he maneuvered slowly, with great intent and purpose. Stepping close and sliding one arm around her waist. Feeling the heat of her body, noticing her labored breathing. He bent one knee to fit between the two of hers before wrapping his other arm around her back, slowly pressing the solidness of his chest against the softness of hers. Her head tilted up. Her lips waiting just below his own. Like the start of a whirlpool, the blood in his head began to circle, threatening to take him under.

His eyes darted away from her face and around the room. "What?" he heard Annabelle's soft rustle of laughter. "Who are you looking for?" she asked.

"Your father," he confessed, then drew his attention back to her upturned face. "God, you're beautiful," he sighed. "But that guy scares me." His gaze shot out around them again.

Annabelle tucked her forehead against his chest. She was laughing at him but it couldn't be helped. He was dying to kiss her and just wasn't willing to ruin the moment by worrying about her daddy as he did. Luckily, there was no sign of the man. But as relief started to flow, he caught movement out of the corner of his eye. The WTF, you've-got-to-be-kidding-me kind.

He cleared his throat. "Annabelle," he said, causing her to look up in surprise. "The thing you are about to find out about me? I've got a temper."

She saw them then. Brooks, Vance and three others moving in their direction.

"I swear to God, if one of them so much as hints at breaking in on this dance, it's gonna get ugly."

She looked between him and the approaching band of buffoons. "Now might be a good time for that test drive," she said.

She took his hand and quickly led him away, bobbing and weaving through the couples slow dancing, heading straight toward the band. *God, how great is this woman?* They turned left at the stage edge, stooping low in front of all the dancers until they hit the outskirts of the crowd, then shot left again and broke into a run toward the far back door. When they hit the hallway, it was less crowded, and there was no sign of Brooks or Vance. Annabelle motioned for him to follow her to the right and then down a set of stairs. The music and party chatter kept receding as they descended, lingering over their heads as a heavy beat when they crossed back under the party and moved down a long, dimly-lit hallway that traversed the back of the clubhouse.

At the sight of the exit doors, Annabelle started laughing and broke into a run. Duncan followed in chase, hitting the door along with her and bounding up a short flight of concrete steps, free at last.

After working up a sweat on the dance floor, he found cool relief in the frigid night air. Annabelle continued to laugh, saying, "I can't believe we just ran away from them." She turned to Duncan, walking backwards into the light cast from a street lamp at the entrance to the parking lot. "Like playing hide and seek when we were kids."

Duncan allowed his steps to slow into a lazy gait, enjoying the scene before him. Annabelle flushed with excitement, her eyes sparkling, her cheeks rosy, that dazzling smile turned on full wattage and directed right at him. The light behind her showing through her white gossamer gown giving him a full view of just how little she wore beneath it. In two quick steps he caught her up in his arms and pressed her to him, thinking he might owe Brooks and Vance a little gratitude for forcing them out here, finally alone under the dark of night. Because he was now going to be able to do the one thing he'd been thinking about for most of the day.

Drive Annabelle's car.

"Aww, damn it to hell," he uttered shaking his head. "And it was such a clean getaway, too."

"What?" she laughed at him. "What could possibly be wrong now?"

"Besides the fact that for the second time today you are standing in the freezing cold wearing next to nothing? We need your car keys, Danica Patrick. Unless you have them strapped to your thigh, I'm guessing they are back inside, tucked into some flimsy little purse."

"Ooh," she said, backing out of his hold and turning toward the parking lot. "There is so much you have left to learn, Officer Friendly," she said, her voice trailing behind her. He caught up with her in time to hear, "We always leave the doors unlocked and the keys under the driver's side mat."

The idea left him dumbstruck as he halted and simply stared after her. Finally he shrugged, "I guess that's good to know. In case I ever need to make a quick getaway."

Impressed that her big bad muscle car was tucked into the end of a row, protecting at least one side from dings, he herded her around to the passenger side and opened the door, helping her in. The bitter cold was starting to seep into his awareness and he would have felt sorry for any Greek Goddess draped only in chiffon if it weren't for the saliva-producing way her nipples responded.

He shut the door and practically growled as he headed to the driver's side.

The inside of the machine was spacious due to its wide, low ride, but the leather bucket seats molded around his thighs, supporting him front to back. He started her up with a roar, and gave the gas a punch just to hear it again. He smiled the exhilarated smile of a kid strapping himself into the latest high-tech roller coaster. Thank God whatever weather system the newscasters had been yammering on about hadn't started yet, because this was gonna be good.

After adjusting the mirrors and fastening his seat belt, he cautiously maneuvered Annabelle's baby out of the parking space, down the lot and out onto the long front drive of the Henderson Country Club. He hit the gas and felt the power surge throw him back as the Camaro went from zero to sixty in one crazy nanosecond.

He was braking before his thoughts could catch up to him, and sat for a moment at the end of the driveway, wondering why the hell he didn't have one of these. Finally he turned his head toward Annabelle and said, "Awesome." She simply nodded.

He fumbled in his jacket pocket for his cell phone and handed it to her. "Call Brooks," he said. "Tell him I wanna open her up along Lake Road. See if any of his cop buddies are patrolling there this time of night."

"Really? You want me to call Brooks and tell him where we are?"

"Haven't we had enough tickets today, Little Miss Speedy Gonzales?"

"Are you kidding me? Brooks will be calling everybody on duty to nail your ass coming and going. You'd be handing him the revenge he needs after you won the bet today."

Duncan stared at Annabelle, open mouthed.

"At least that's what I'd do." She flicked her shoulder. "But it's your money," she said, starting to dial.

Duncan grabbed the phone out of her hands. "It's exactly what I'd do, too," he muttered. "And what Brooks would do," he assured her. "And did I just hear the word 'ass' come out of your mouth?" he said, stuffing the phone back in his pocket. "The Queen of Etiquette?" he said, putting the Camaro in gear and moving out onto the open road. "Or was that the hot babe in the Auto Mechanics Club talking?"

Annabelle just smiled into the night whizzing by her. "Take your pick," she said.

I want both.

It was then that the thrill turned from the drive to what might be found at the destination.

CHAPTER EIGHT

Lake Road was the perfect place to open her up, but Annabelle knew that speed was one thrill, and handling another. So after Duncan hit somewhere around one hundred-twenty on the speedometer, Annabelle directed him to a winding country road leading up a small pass to a park that overlooked the lake. The back and forth turns could have been taken with a bit more speed in the light of day, but Duncan's expressions and occasional outbursts assured her that he was having a good time playing with her car.

The road dumped into a small parking lot, which was apparently just large enough for Duncan to gun the engine, spin them around and skid into a stop. All of which was a little more daredevil than Duncan probably had intended, producing a short scream from Annabelle and some wide eyes and heavy breathing from him as the car settled beneath them.

"Oh my God!" "That was close!" they said at the same time.

"I got a little carried away," he said sheepishly.

"Believe me, I understand," she assured him. "Would you mind taking off your coat before we start back?"

Duncan looked down at his tuxedo jacket. "I am so sorry," he said, quickly stripping the coat from his arms. "You must be freezing."

"No," she said, folding his jacket and holding it over the back seat. She let it drop behind them.

"No?" he said, his eyes shifting back and forth between hers.

She shook her head as she reached for his right hand and started to unfasten the cufflink she found at his wrist. Duncan watched in silence as she dropped it into the cup holder. But when she leaned over him and started to unfasten the other one, he dragged in a slow breath and caught the back of her head in the palm of his hand. She finished pulling the cufflink free just as he turned her face to his.

"Annabelle," he whispered, his breath labored. "Annabelle, I...."

At a loss for words he brought his other hand up and captured the side of her face, pressing her back a little before his mouth caught up to his hands. He pressed his lips to hers in a slow, soft kiss.

It was just a tease, a tender touch, but oh how it shot rockets of desire through her body. He angled his head and kissed her again, this time allowing his tongue to sweep gently across her upper lip and then her lower one. He turned his head the other way and Annabelle's hands moved up of their own volition to grab onto his wrists as his mouth toyed again with delicious tenderness.

"Annabelle," he whispered, balancing his forehead against hers. "I was trying to hold out until midnight."

Deliberately licking her lips, she whispered back, "I got tired of waiting."

"I was trying to mind my manners," he grunted as he hauled her over to the driver's side, and settled her onto his lap. "Something I'm aware the Keeper of the Debutantes is all about." With her back to the door and her legs draped over him and the center console, he hit the seat adjustment button to move them back from the steering wheel as far as possible.

Annabelle's fingers started in on his bow tie, pulling it loose with expert hands. "First my jacket. Then my cufflinks. Now my tie? What am I? Your little Ken doll?"

Annabelle stopped her fingers on the second stud of his shirt, slanting her head to consider. "No. You're more like my Officer Friendly action figure. And I've been dying to see you without a shirt ever since this afternoon when you wrapped me in your coat and pulled me up against this chest." She rubbed her hands down his shirt, over his pectoral muscles and his rib cage then back up and over his shoulders. She stopped at his biceps and squeezed.

Duncan watched her ogle him, his grin spreading from ear to ear. "I guess a girl who drives a muscle car might have an appreciation for...." His words fell off while he moved his fingers into Annabelle's hair. "I had this crazy urge this afternoon, too," he said slowly, as if remembering. "I wanted to run my hand through your hair. Like this," he said threading his fingers up the back of her scalp. "And then pull you close," he whispered as he did. "And kiss you," he went on as he touched her lips with short, soft kisses. "Like I meant it," he breathed before he deepened the kiss.

The thrill of his tongue finally demanding its way into her mouth shot a branding heat throughout her chest and down the center of her rib cage. Her body grew heavy and warm and then seemed to fade away. Her mind fell into a blissful state of semi-consciousness while she kissed Duncan James.

Like rising through the fog of a dream and entering slowly back into a state of awareness, Annabelle found herself in Duncan's arms, her body tingling in arousal, his mouth trailing its way from her lips, down her throat and over to the sensitive spot just above her clavicle. She felt his tongue swirl across the indentation there and his hands moving up on both sides of her rib cage, his thumbs brushing the underside of her breasts at first…then finally moving across the peaks of her nipples.

She heard a sound escape, though she was unaware of making it, so focused on her core being melted, tipped, and now cascading down to pool at the southernmost region of her body.

"I want…." she started, eyes closed, licking her lips. "I need to…." she tried again, but had no ability to find the right words. "Here," she finally breathed, gripping the back of his seat and leveraging herself around Duncan's legs. She pulled at her gown, gathering it high so her legs could straddle his, bringing them face to face. She eased her body down to his lap and bit her bottom lip when the throbbing aching need of her met the rock-solid heat of him.

Duncan rolled his pelvis in response. His hands slid down to grip her hips. "Jesus Christ," he cursed as he rocked himself against her again. His hands slid under her gown and up her parted thighs, feeling their way to the soft curve of her behind, moving her forward at the same time as he ground himself against her. His mouth sought hers and she feasted on his lips, tilting her pelvis to help create more friction.

The deliciousness of her body moving against his, of his arms tightening around her, of the way their lips played, the way their tongues tangled, the joy of being alive and having found the One bubbled up inside Annabelle and it all came out in a yummy, humming sort of groaning approval that vibrated against his lips.

"I know," he breathed, a hand coming up and sweeping the hair back from her face. "This feels really…." He kissed her again. "Really…." He got lost in her lips, and his hands groped around for purchase between the sides of her thighs, her lower back, sometimes skimming her aching breasts but not settling anywhere for long. Finally, he set both hands on either side of her face and put some distance between their lips. He looked at her, then closed his eyes, panting.

"This…." he started, opening his eyes and staring at her seriously. "We…" His chest heaved with a large intake of breath as he managed to continue, "are not making this a one-night stand."

Annabelle leaned back a little. "Are you asking me out on a second date?"

He nodded, still holding his hands to her head. "Are you accepting?"

She nodded back.

"I'm serious," he told her.

"I believe you," she said.

His hands fell from her face in exasperation. "And I probably am going to have to turn in my Man Card for this, but I have no intention of making love to you for the first time in this car. It just would…" his voice began to trail off, "set the wrong tone for a relationship." He turned his head and looked out into the darkness.

The silence pounded heavy and long, matching Annabelle's heartbeat. She wanted to respond with a gift of words equal to what he'd just bestowed upon her. But her mind could find nothing worthy. Emotion swelled within her and before she could lean into him, he turned his face back and barked, "Don't you debutantes have a five date rule or something?"

She nodded briskly and saw his features soften. Inches apart, he had to have noticed the tears in her eyes. "We should," she sniffed, nodding again. "We really should." She eased herself down against him, pressing her cheek against his shoulder.

His arms closed snugly around her as he said, "So let's count this up. We have tonight, date number one. Your daddy asked me over tomorrow for the Rose Bowl, so maybe we can count that as date number two." Annabelle simply snuggled down lower. "Tomorrow night we both will be back in Raleigh and I'm thinking I'd like to take you to dinner, if that's all right." She nodded her head against his chest. "That's date number three."

He rubbed his cheek. "Friday night is always a good movie date night," he said. "You free this Friday?" He tucked his chin to look down at her and she nodded against him again. "Okay, good. Date number four."

A comfortable silence settled around them, the heater still pouring out warmth, the headlights still shining on the road back down the hill. When Duncan started to talk, it was as if he were constructing a poetic invitation. "For date number five," he breathed, tilting his head and kissing the soft spot behind her ear, "I will discover, through my own devices, your favorite flower and present you with a bouquet when I arrive to pick you up. We'll take my car—which is not as fast as this one but a little more luxurious—to The Capital Grille where we'll enjoy a steak dinner by candlelight at a very secluded table. I'll order a fine cabernet and we'll share the chocolate soufflé for dessert. And while we're at dinner, we'll make plans for Valentine's Day weekend. And then," he said, leaning down and catching her lips up with his, "I will take you home and make love to you," he said between kisses, "all…night…long."

CHAPTER NINE

Their absence wasn't noticed until Annabelle and Duncan arrived back at the party hand in hand, moonstruck by all accounts. If anyone had been watching—and no one was, due to the shenanigans on stage—they'd notice that the kiss they shared at midnight was both hungry and eager. In high spirits, watching Annabelle say goodbye to friends and relatives as the party began to dwindle, Duncan's only pang of uncertainty came when he overheard Annabelle tell one of her debutantes about instituting a "five date rule". He had a sinking feeling that that whole thing was going to come back and bite him in the ass.

Duncan's concern about getting along with Mr. Devine and gaining his favor was short-lived. The man seemed genuinely delighted to have a bit more testosterone around the house watching football during date number two. It was the Devine women who threw Duncan a curve ball from the moment he arrived.

It was hard to miss that Mrs. D was all grins and sighs whenever Duncan spoke about anything. And likewise, Grace—no longer the fairy princess but still a knockout in her faded blue jeans–stared at Duncan wide-eyed in wonder for most of the day. Tess... Well, Tess didn't pay him much mind, though when she did deem to acknowledge his presence, it was always with a great amount of personal satisfaction. As if Annabelle had told her that he did, indeed, kiss as well as Lewis Kampmueller—and that in some way Tess was pleased for her sister.

Annabelle, herself, was simply *more*.

More sporty—in jeans and a Carolina blue v-neck sweater—her red hair in a high pony-tail with a twist that bounced with so much life he couldn't help but tug on it.

More playful—as she interacted with him and her family. Her knowledge of football and sports in general, setting her apart from the other females.

More handsy—touching him casually in front of her parents and in more shocking ways when she pulled him into the kitchen to prepare a plethora of snacks.

She was a handful, this Annabelle Devine, stealing kisses and insinuating about Saturday night every chance she got.

The complete package was more to his liking than Duncan could have dreamed. Annabelle was a rose, with more soft and intriguing petals than he could count. He definitely did not want to blow this. But after stopping in at the Bennetts' before heading back to Raleigh, he began to worry that he already had.

"Aren't you a little young for needing Viagra?" Vance started in on him by the beer refrigerator out in the garage. "I mean, just because you can't get it up doesn't mean you have to ruin things for the rest of us."

Duncan squinted at the fool in front of him. "What the hell are you talking about, Evans?"

Vance just looked disgusted and took a swig from his bottle.

"He's just a little pissed at this five date rule," Brooks offered.

"Oh shit."

"Oh shit is right," Vance agreed, popping Duncan's chest with the lip of his long-neck bottle. "I don't care if you want to play the gentleman for Ms. Devine or if you're covering up the fact that you've been neutered. Leave the fucking rest of us out of your insanity, Dunc. Some of us are interested in getting laid before the fifth date. Before any date," Vance spat.

"How the hell did this get out?"

"Oh, bro. It's out. It's out and alive and crawling all over the place," Brooks said. "The women of Henderson are loving this. They'll probably have a statue erected in your honor. Anyone with a daughter is singing your praises right about now. Of course," he said,

taking a swig of beer, "anybody with a pair of balls would like to cut yours off."

Duncan squeezed his eyes shut and stood contemplating all the ramifications of his conversation with Annabelle. And the one he focused on was the horror of Annabelle finding out the actual truth. Because for someone who prided himself on valuing truth above all else, he'd gone and bent it twice in one day. And he knew himself and his temper well enough to know that, had Annabelle been the one doing the truth bending, he'd be walking away and not looking back.

He knew he should keep it to himself, but the guilt had started to grow the moment he'd seen the emotion in her eyes. He couldn't do it. He couldn't keep this in. He had to tell somebody.

"Look," he said, releasing a huge breath. "I wasn't trying to be a gentleman. The truth is, I just couldn't find the damn zipper on her dress."

By the time Duncan stood on the doorstep of Annabelle's condominium in Raleigh, ready for date number three, he'd considered and rejected a million ways to tell her the truth.

What he'd said was true. He damn well didn't want a one-night stand. And he had no intention of making love in that crazy-ass car of hers. But he was only a man for God's sake, and a weak one at that. Things had heated up faster than he could keep ahead of, and his saving grace was that her dress had zipped up the side, not the back. So he'd fallen back on Plan A and told her the truth. But when she didn't respond, he'd felt vulnerable and threw out the five date rule bullshit. And now she'd gone and told the debutantes and who knew who the hell else. No wonder her mother and sisters were looking at him with big ol' eyes all afternoon.

He wanted Annabelle to fall in love with him, but not under false pretenses. He had to tell her the truth.

But date number three at the sports bar went so well—eating hamburgers and discovering more and more about each other—including a bunch of mutual friends—that Duncan literally forgot the dark cloud hanging over everything. Who would have guessed that a red-headed Southern belle liked to ski the double black diamond slopes, or had her own bookie?

The date went later than either of them planned and for the second night in a row, at the stroke of midnight, there was a kiss that set off fireworks.

❧

OMG falling fast. Annabelle texted Grace and Tess the next day. *Sending pictures of possible lingerie for Saturday night. Stand by.*

Annabelle snapped pictures of a combination camisole and boy-shorts, nude in color and adorned in French lace, a baby pink bra and panty set, and a sexy but fun black strapless negligee that tied under the bust with a big red bow.

Your signature white? Grace texted.

Wearing a killer white dress, she texted back. Her phone rang and Tess was on the other end.

"I like the red bow. Like he's opening a gift," Tess teased.

"Yeah." Annabelle smiled into the phone. "I thought so too. It's flirty. I just want to make sure it's not too flirty. Too much."

"Annabelle, you are planning to consummate this relationship, right? I don't think anything is too flirty at this point."

"I know," she said, moving to a corner of the store so her voice wouldn't be overheard. "It's just that Duncan is such a gentleman and I basically threw myself at him the other night. I'm nervous. Everything about him, us, seems so good. What if it doesn't hold up in the bedroom? What if he expects me to be all prim and proper? Or worse—what if *he's* all prim and proper?"

"You told me there was plenty of chemistry."

"On my side, yeah. My body is having its own nuclear meltdown. But he was the one who put on the brakes. I was a sure thing after one long kiss. I was the aggressor. What if that turned him off?"

"Little sister, this is music to my ears. I didn't think you had it in you."

"Oh, it's in me. Apparently Duncan brings it out with a vengeance. I just…I just don't want to be the only one losing control. I want him to be, you know, crazy for me."

"Trust me on this," Tess said. "I've seen the way he looks at you. You have nothing to worry about. Buy the lingerie and call me on Sunday." Tess hung up.

Annabelle looked at her phone. "And then there is that pesky little detail of how we met," she said to herself.

Annabelle had an agenda all worked out for their movie date. Come clean, then seduce the hell out of Duncan.

Duncan, on the other hand, had his own agenda. Keep his hands as far away from Annabelle as he possibly could. After their last date, where he had to bite his own tongue in order not to beg her to let him escort her inside, he was determined to make it to tomorrow night. If nothing else, he hoped by then she'd be as horny as he when he told her the truth about the five date rule. He was fully prepared to give her the full-court press seduction and push not taking no for an answer within an inch of propriety.

During the action-packed thriller, when Annabelle's hand crept onto his thigh, creating the beginnings of a raging hard-on, he intertwined his fingers with hers and relentlessly held on to them for the rest of the movie. The only time he let himself go was when he pressed her up against the car door and took her mouth with his own, letting her feel the effect she had on him—promising her that tomorrow night would be worth the wait.

It wasn't until he was alone in bed that he remembered Annabelle saying, "I have something I need to tell you," right before he'd cut her off by maneuvering his way into her arms.

To Annabelle, the beginning of date number five was as poetic as Duncan had described. Her mouth watered when she opened the door to find him looking ridiculously handsome in a traditional blue blazer and gorgeous lavender Façonnable shirt and tie. She'd worn her hair up just in case he did bring her favorite flower, so she was delighted when he presented her with a gardenia, and promptly added it to her coiffure. Their elegant circular booth at The Capital Grille was cozy and secluded with an already decanted bottle of Rubicon cabernet awaiting their arrival. When she found the second gardenia artistically arranged among the votive candles, she fell in love. And as they sat side by side, enjoying a glass of wine after first indulging in a Stoli Doli, Capital Grille's signature cocktail, Annabelle was smiling inside and out because Duncan James couldn't keep his hands off her.

"When I first saw you tonight…" Duncan whispered, kissing the indentation beneath her ear, his fingers brushing tendrils of hair back from her neck, "you took my breath away." His mouth trailed down her throat. "You'd think I'd get used to it because it happens every time I see you." He brushed his lips and tongue over the tender spot at the base of her neck that so fascinated him. "Annabelle," he breathed, "I've been longing to bite you right here ever since New Year's Eve."

She tipped her head giving him better access, pressing a hand against his thigh in response to the heat and sensation. "That's good to know," she whispered. "I worried I may have been too forward."

He choked a stilted laugh and sat up, handing over her wine glass. "Finish your wine," he said. "I have a confession to make."

She eyed him suspiciously, taking a sip. "Is it so bad you have to ply me with fabulous wine? I know you're not married," she teased. But as their waiter approached, Duncan silently waved him off. That's when her stomach sank. "Okay, now I'm getting worried."

"I want to straighten out a misconception, before…before we… you know."

"Have sex," she supplied.

Duncan leveled her with that reprimanding stare. The one that let her know she was precariously close to crossing a line. His body became a fortress. One strong arm resting across the booth behind her, his broad shoulders hemming her in at the side, and his other arm tense on the table in front of her. He spoke in that quiet no-nonsense baritone that made her insides weep with longing and anticipation.

"Annabelle." God, she loved how he said her name. "Every word I told you in your car New Year's Eve was true. I wanted a second date. I wanted a chance at a relationship. I did not want a one-night stand." His upper body angled closer, causing her heart to pound. His gaze drifted to her mouth for a moment, then back to her eyes. "But with you on my lap, I was perfectly willing to take advantage of the situation anyway." His voice dropped to a whisper. "At one point, all I could think about was stripping you naked and,"—his gaze dropped briefly to her thighs—"sliding you down onto me."

Her eyes went wide as every bit of pent-up desire slid south and turned hot and moist. Her breath caught in her chest, her heart pounding enough to make her pulse points throb. She licked her lips and Duncan leaned closer.

"The truth is, the only thing that stopped me was that I couldn't find the zipper on your gown. It was much later that night when I realized the damn thing zipped up the side."

The sexual tension was too taut for her to laugh. The only thing she could think to say was, "Oh?"

Duncan eyed her mouth again before leaning back. "I got frustrated when I couldn't find the zipper," he said, moving his hand off the table and on to her thigh, "and that made me stop and realize where we were heading. I didn't want to give you the impression that sex was all I wanted. I didn't want to do anything to embarrass you or make you want to avoid me the next morning. But the point is," he said eyeing her heavily, "had the zipper been in the back where it normally is, I wouldn't have stopped. And this whole five date rule? Complete bullshit."

Annabelle felt her head nodding but her mind had shut down after the words "sliding you down onto me." With her body vibrating so intensely, the only thing she could think about was how she had to tell him the truth about how they met. Her heart squeezed at the thought of his rejection. God, she didn't want to ruin this.

Finding no way to avoid the inevitable, she finally pointed to his glass of wine. "Drink up," she insisted.

Duncan looked a little stunned. A little confused.

"Drink up," she repeated, motioning him toward the wine with her hand. "Because if that's the extent of your confession, I assure you it's a sonnet compared to what I have to tell you."

"Tell me?" he questioned, releasing her thigh and reaching for his glass. "Wait! Before you say anything. Are we good? I mean, are you okay with what I just said?"

She licked her lips and leaned in to kiss him, whispering, "I'm *very* okay with *everything* you just said."

His relief turned into a big, sultry grin. "Okay then." He took up his wine and downed what was left like it was cheap beer at a keg party, then all but smacked his glass on the table. "Your turn."

Tears threatened as Annabelle described how her father had

overheard Brooks bet Duncan he couldn't give her a speeding ticket. How he'd come home that night and told her all about it. And then how he'd recommended she play along so she could meet Duncan and see if he was the kind of guy she'd be interested in.

While Annabelle talked, she saw Duncan's expression shift the moment he figured out where her story was heading. He sat there in silence through its entirety, staring at her. When he started to drum his fingers on the table, she wrapped it up, figuring no amount of talking was going to put the cat back in the bag.

"Are you done?" he said, his eyebrows lifting. Annabelle nodded a weak little nod, terrified of his next words.

Duncan turned to the waiter hovering in the distance. "Check, please."

"Oh my God. Duncan, no!" Annabelle pleaded, throwing her hands up to his shoulders trying to turn him around to look at her. "Please, don't be mad…." she went on, becoming aware of a suspicious shaking under her hands as he turned around. Laughing.

She threw him her very best pout, but he said, "You deserved that. You and your father. I cannot believe I was set up."

"Believe it," she groaned. "And it was brilliant…all except for the part where I started to fall for you. Then it became weird and twisted and this big fat lie that I had to live with—"

She saw the poor waiter scurry off again as Duncan pulled her close and shut her up with one long, hard kiss. Her toes literally curled. "You started to fall for me?" he asked against her lips, sounding very pleased.

Annabelle simply nodded against him.

"Okay, then. How 'bout that steak?"

CHAPTER TEN

"Nervous?"

Annabelle responded with a quick smile as Duncan unlocked the door. Yeah, she was nervous. The two of them were never at a loss for words, but the drive home had been noticeably quiet. Just like their walk from the car to Duncan's townhouse.

And now, she thought, now they were literally standing on a threshold.

"Come here," he said, reaching out, taking one of her hands and slowly moving it up to his shoulder. He stepped in like he was pulling her close for a slow dance when her feet came out from under her and, like Scarlett O'Hara, she found herself airborne and being carried off in the arms of her own Rhett Butler.

"Duncan James," she said, "you've been sweeping me off my feet all week."

Once inside, he backed up against the door, closing it with his backside, and asked her to lock it by throwing the deadbolt. Then he said, "How 'bout I give you a tour in the morning?" She simply nodded as that delicious nervous angst bloomed inside her chest.

He walked to the stairs and set her feet down on the first step so they stood more or less eye to eye. His hands moved into her hair on either side of her face. "I'm crazy about you, Annabelle Devine." With exquisite concentration, he took his time kissing her lower lip, lightly running his tongue across the upper one. "I want you in my bed something awful," he drawled, his Southern accent growing heavy, his voice going sleepy. He trailed his lips across her jaw line. "I'm completely healthy," he assured her, moving down her neck toward that one little spot she was growing so fond of. "I'm prepared. I'll protect you," he promised, his mouth settling on top of her shoulder then trailing a path to the sensitive place where he nipped at her flesh.

Moving a hand to the banister and another to her hip, Duncan nudged her backward up the next step while his mouth played again with hers. "There's no zipper on this dress," he said between kisses, moving them further up the steps. The pressure of his hand on her hip was tantalizing. "So I'm gonna watch you take it off," he said pulling her firmly against him halfway up the stairs.

His tongue slid into her mouth and plundered. Annabelle moaned against him as the wave of passion tossed her under its magnificent surge. Gone again was conscious thought. Her mind drifted to another dimension while her body remained anchored by the onslaught of chemical combustion. Her breasts felt engorged and begged to be touched. Her thighs quivered with need. Her tiny lace thong grew damp from arousal. And just as it had been on New Year's Eve, she longed to feel the firm, steely heat of him rubbing against the soft throbbing ache of her.

"Annabelle…baby," Duncan whispered in her ear. "Take your dress off for me, please. Right here. Right now." He held her by her shoulders until she was steady. Her dress, created by rings of fabric, needed to be pulled over her head. So she licked her lips and watched his expression through lowered lashes as she slowly drew the gardenia from her hair and let it drop to her feet. She noticed his jaw tighten as she deliberately removed the tiny hairpins one by one, making a great show of letting them fall from her fingertips. She watched him swallow when the tight white fabric started to inch up her thighs, saw that his eyes were trained on the apex of her legs. She hesitated on the brink of exposing her pink lace lingerie, causing Duncan's eyes to flick from the tops of her bare thighs to her face and back again.

When she continued to stall, he closed his eyes and licked his lips. "Sweet Jesus, Annabelle. I swear to God, one slice down the middle is all it will take." He started reaching for his back pocket but froze to watch Annabelle pull the dress up and over the moist heat hidden behind her pink lace thong…then fully expose her hour glass figure and lacy push-up bra. She drew the dress over her head, then shook out her red curls and combed her fingers through her hair before tossing the ball of fabric to land behind him on the foyer floor.

Duncan growled as his jacket hit the floor. And, as he loosened his tie, he backed her up the next two steps while pulling his shirttail from his pants and unbuttoning the cuffs. "Still wanna see me with my shirt off?" he asked, stalking her.

Annabelle could only nod, reaching out to steady herself with the banister. Her red heels started to slip, so she took one off and then the other as he backed her up the steps. When she looked up again, Duncan's chest was exposed. And boy, oh boy was it *magnificent.* She stifled most of a squeak as her eyes feasted on his tanned and muscled torso with its sexy smattering of curly dark hair which dipped and narrowed, disappearing beyond the waistband of his slacks. Her eyes drifted there just in time to watch Duncan loosen the buckle and pull his belt out of its loops with menacing slowness. He held it over the banister and let it drop to the floor below.

Annabelle came to a dead stop short of the top of the stairs. Her eyes took in the length and breadth of the ill-concealed hard-on behind Duncan's pants. She glanced up only when she heard him say, "You are welcome to lick your lips all you'd like."

She felt her face flush and was at a loss for a pithy comeback, suddenly realizing she was in way over her head. Duncan. Older and obviously more experienced. She. Four years his junior and far, far less experienced, she was sure. And this—her heart caught in her chest—this meant so much. This…being with him, meant… everything.

Frantic, she turned to run from the realization. Run from the emotion boiling up inside her. Run from the fact that she was in love with Duncan James and couldn't bear to make one false move and jeopardize it all. She sprinted up the rest of the steps and ran down the hall, but Duncan grabbed her up by the waist and hauled her in the opposite direction saying, "The bedroom is this way."

Short of kicking and screaming, she flailed enough so that he put her down as soon as he managed to get her through the door. Then he shut them inside, turned his back to the door and folded his arms across his chest. Annabelle's breathing was heavy and labored and it cost her every ounce of courage she had to meet Duncan's eyes.

"You freaking out?"

"Little bit."

He nodded. Then looked down at the floor. Realizing he still had his shoes on, he toed them off. "Okay," he said through a thick release of breath, running a hand through his hair before looking back up at Annabelle. He spread his arms in quandary. "Well…you look beautiful," he said, indicating her partially naked state with a quick gesture before reaching up and rubbing his jaw.

"It's just…." Annabelle started. "It's just that…." But the swell of emotion grew so intense that the only place she could imagine finding solace was in Duncan's arms. So she moved to him, wrapped her arms around his waist and laid her cheek against his chest. His strong arms engulfed her upper body and held her tight. "It's just that it's all fun and games until someone gets hurt," she whimpered.

Duncan rubbed her back and kissed the top of her head. "No one is going to get hurt."

"You don't know that."

"Yes," he said, lifting her chin so he could see her eyes, "I do."

She believed him. She trusted he believed what he was saying and that was all she could ask. She reached up and placed a hand at the back of his neck, coaxing his lips to hers. Tentatively she pressed her tongue between his lips to meld with his own and offered up not only a sweet kiss, but her trust and belief as well. Both arms came up to circle his neck and she stood on tiptoe as he pressed her pelvis to his, letting their heat meld there as well.

"Touch me, please," Duncan breathed. "God knows it's all I can think about." He took her head in his hands and devoted exquisite attention to her mouth while her hands drifted over his shoulders, slid down his chest and worked together to unfasten the waistband and unzip his pants. "God, yes," he moaned into her mouth, kissing her with greater intensity as she slid one hand down between his pants and his boxer-briefs that covered the taut, firm shaft of his erection.

He pushed himself against the heel of her palm as she slid it down the length of him, and then groaned his approval when she used her fingers to massage his balls through the fabric. His lips kept their connection as he removed his pants. Then he took her hand and moved it inside the elastic band of his shorts and she followed his lead, slowly exposing his erection as the heat of her hand came in contact with the engorged shaft of his cock. He sighed her name in appreciation.

As his legs worked to disengage his boxers, Duncan slid the straps of Annabelle's bra off her shoulders, biting the smooth skin at the side of her neck. He unhooked her bra and pulled it down between them, his mouth eagerly following his hands to her aching breasts. She sighed, closing her eyes, biting her lower lip as she guided his hands to use more pressure. Her need swelled in delight and she rocked her pelvis against his shaft, stroking both of them where they needed it most.

Her legs instinctively circled Duncan's waist when he lifted her up, backing her to his bed where he lifted one knee, guiding them both on to the top of his comforter. Annabelle slid backward to the head of the bed, digging her fingers into the end of the comforter and pushing it under her body as Duncan helped drag it down beyond them. He laid her down, her head on his pillow and took his time to look his fill of her naked breasts, narrow waist, and long shapely legs.

"How the hell did I get so lucky?" he asked, sliding one hand up and down the side of her body as his eyes roamed freely. "Underneath all your stylish perfection, there is this sinfully, smokin' hot body." He lowered his head, closed his mouth over a nipple and sucked hard, causing Annabelle to gasp and buck her pelvis. He covered her lower body with his own, feasting on her breasts while drawing her hands up over her head.

His own hands slid back down languidly, caressing the sensitive insides of her arms, the ticklish depression of her underarms, the rounded sides of her breasts, and the indentation of her waist before tucking themselves under her back and massaging her buttocks. "I've been dying to get my hands on your shapely derrière," he said leaving a trail of kisses down her stomach and over her navel as his hands fondled her hips and rear-end.

He pulled the silky threads of her G-string down her hips and off her legs. Annabelle closed her eyes, feeling the contrast as cool air hit her warm, wet pubic hair, leaving every part of her exposed. Duncan traced his thumb through the thick of it, making her body bow when it slid over her clitoris and continued down her slick center. "So perfect," he said, his breath tantalizing the engorged nerve endings. His mouth lowered and he lovingly kissed her right where she could feel it most.

"Oh baby, there's so much I long to do to you," he moaned, lifting up and crawling forward over her body. "But I can't get what you did to me the other night out of my head," he said looking into her eyes. "Here," he offered his hand and helped her sit up. Then he moved back against the headboard and fumbled with a condom before taking her hand and bringing her to him.

"Just like you did before," he begged, clasping her hips and maneuvering her on to his lap. "Rub yourself against me," he pleaded as she slid her body along the back side of his erect shaft. "God yes," he breathed, his head thrown back as Annabelle started to rub her aching center up and down the long length of his cock, her body providing lubricant for the condom. "I fantasized about this," he said bringing his gaze down between them to watch the action. "Every night since." He cupped her ass with his hands and set the rhythm for the both of them. "Feel good?" he asked when Annabelle started to moan.

"So good," she said, closing her eyes, licking her lips. He smiled. She could hear it when he spoke.

"That mouth of yours is one hell of a turn-on," he said, moving her body a little faster. She tilted her hips and pressed harder, targeting her swollen nub. Duncan's hips started to pump causing an "even better" to spill from her lips.

"You like this, baby?" Duncan asked, his breath coming faster. His fingers gripping her ass tighter. His cock sliding quickly within the folds of her flesh. "Is this what you needed? Finish what you started New Year's Eve, Annabelle. Come on, baby. Come for me," he breathed, "Come for me so I can take us where we both want to go."

He reached between them to press his cock hard against her. When Annabelle first started to spasm and shake, he moved his thumb over her nub and manipulated her into a soul-wrenching orgasm. And as the hollow need inside her grew desperate to be filled, he lifted her up and then slid her down, sheathing his erection.

Another orgasm erupted immediately, causing her body to go loose everywhere except where it counted for Duncan. Her internal muscles milked him hard, setting off a wild chain of events.

Duncan pushed Annabelle to her back while she still came, whimpering his name, squeezing his cock inside the very core of her body. "Holy shi—" he began, but the blood drained from his head down to his groin, erasing all thought. His hips worked like a piston, ferociously fucking the girl of his dreams. Every muscle from his toes to his forehead strained, his shoulders and neck were rigid, his jaw clenched. He heard himself grunt louder and louder, out of control with every pump, until his entire body shook uncontrollably with a long, hard climax.

"Holy Mother of God," he panted, lying on top of her, sweaty and spent.

Moments later, still breathing heavily, he reached for Annabelle's hand and squeezed it.

She squeezed back.

Finally finding the strength to move, he rolled off and sprawled flat on his back, both their heads at the end of the bed. "Annabelle, sweetheart," he whispered, his heart rate still off the chart, "I'm afraid you're gonna have to marry me." His other hand collapsed on top of his stomach and he closed his eyes as Annabelle rose up on an elbow to peer down at him.

Through labored breathing he told her again, "You're gonna have to marry me, baby." He opened his eyes and wiped sweat from them. "Because there is no doubt you have just ruined me for all other women. And, more importantly," he went on, "I know damn well there isn't a condom in this world built strong enough to survive a fuck like that."

He glanced over as Annabelle choked out a laugh at his ungentlemanly choice of words. Giving his spent body a long, cool once-over, she shrugged a shoulder. "Okay," she said before flopping back down and snuggling in against him. "I'll call Daddy."

He smiled at that, his arm going around her, his fingers playing over her deliciously soft skin. And then he smiled broader because he was a lawyer. And although Miss Devine might be somewhat unaware, she'd just entered herself into a verbal contract.

And he had every intention of holding her to it.

Interested in what romance has is in store
for Duncan's friends Brooks and Vance?

GOOD COP
HEROES OF HENDERSON ~ BOOK 1

LIZ KELLY

Good Cop
Heroes of Henderson ~ Book 1

What happens when best friends fall for the same girl?

A Bromance, A Romance
and
A Love Triangle

Local sports heroes Brooks Bennett and Vance Evans are used to being part of a winning team. But when it comes to romance their good cop, bad cop images have them handcuffed. They want a woman's point of view to help unshackle their reputations, and they've picked out one pretty, pony-tailed firecracker to do it.

Lolly DuVal longs for a summer fling that can set off all her bells and whistles. So she agrees to tutor Henderson's hunkiest heroes on what women really want. Now she finds herself caught between two cops and a hard place. And those bells and whistles? They are starting to sound a whole lot more like alarms.

EXCERPT

"Let's face it, bro. You and I have covered a lot of female territory over the years without much to show for it. And up until now that hasn't really bothered me. But now that Duncan and Lewis are racing to the altar and the big 3-0 is breathing down our necks, I think it's time to take a look at that. I mean, I've always thought I'd have kids and a family. Sort of create the environment I was denied growing up. And as Duncan so indelicately pointed out, we need to find women who will have us. And unfortunately I think our reputations have been cemented. We have become the epitome of good cop, bad cop."

"Me being the good cop," Brooks stated.

"Yeah. So somehow I need to become more like you."

"Whatever. It's gonna be a cold day in hell when I start treating women the way you do."

"Fine. Not crazy about the good cop, bad cop analogy? Substitute safe versus sexy."

"Really? Sexy?"

"Well," Vance said, lifting an eyebrow, "I'm certainly not milquetoast."

Brooks planted his ass on the training table Lolly had vacated, shaking himself all over. "*Brrr!* Just saying the word 'sexy' makes me feel ridiculous."

"Yeah, and like I wanna be this town's Golden Boy." Vance broke into his best Brooks Bennett imitation. "Hey, Mrs. Devine! How's your golf game? Really? Well, you hang in there. And give my best to Tess when you speak to her next, will you?" Vance mimicked.

"That is not how I sound."

"That is exactly how you sound to me."

"Well, you can't be me and I refuse to be you."

"Yes, but we can gain a better understanding of where we're lacking and improve in those areas. I need to figure out how to lighten up and get women to wave at me when I walk through town like they do to you."

"And I need to learn how to make their eyes go dark and misty like Lolly's did when she told you, that you had very, very good hands. What the hell was going on in here, you goddamn son of a bitch?"

"Brooks, buddy. That crap is so easy."

"Not for me."

"Which is why, if you go along with my plan, I will reveal to you the secret of my success. Which I learned at the age of fifteen, by the way. It's certainly not rocket science."

"What plan?"

"We help Lolly with her research and she helps us with ours."

"I don't follow."

"She's the tutor."

"No. She's my date."

"Tonight she's your date. Tomorrow she's our tutor."

"Our tutor, how?"

"Man, I don't know. But what I do know is that she was willing to talk about what she didn't want. So maybe she'd be willing to talk about what she does want. It certainly can't hurt to ask. Who else are we gonna get?"

Brooks shrugged. "I don't know. And I see your point, I really do. But I'm hoping this date isn't going to be a one and done."

"Well then…." Vance spread his arms wide. "What could be better than learning about what women want from the woman you actually want?"

"Huh?"

"Trust me. There's no downside here. Let's just talk to her tonight and see if she'd be willing to help us."

"I don't know."

"All right. How 'bout this? I give you one piece of bad cop advice to use on your date tonight. If it works out well for you, and it will, you go along with me on this."

Brooks looked skeptical. "What's the advice?"

"Do we have a deal? Because this is good stuff and frankly, right now, in this town, you are my stiffest competition. I don't want to be giving you pointers and getting nothing in return."

"Jesus, will you just tell me already?"

"Okay." Vance took a breath before speaking in a conspiratorial tone. "Tonight, when you take the Lollypop home, the moment you hit that top step of her momma's porch you shove that lean body of hers right up against the wall and kiss her like you mean it."

Vance let that sink in before he added, "You can thank me in the morning."

∽৵≈৵

Good Cop
Heroes of Henderson ∽ Book 1
by
Liz Kelly

Liz Kelly Books

All of my Heroes of Henderson novels and novellas are complete romances in and of themselves and do not need to be read in any particular order. However, it's a little more fun that way.

Taming Molly and *Tempting Vivi* are part of The DuVal Cousins series showcasing Lolly's Henderson cousins as heroines of their own stories.

Heroes of Henderson full-length Novels

Good Cop
Bad Cop
Top Dog
Tempting Vivi
Under Dog - *Coming in 2015*

Heroes of Henderson Novellas

Playin' Cop
Taming Molly

For more information and excerpts from all my novels, please visit my website: www.LizKellyBooks.com and sign up for my newsletter to learn about future releases.

About the Author

Growing up every summer in a place where *dancing and romancing* are literally part of its theme song, Liz Kelly can't help but be a romantic at heart. And since her favorite author, Kathleen E. Woodiwiss wrote some of the world's greatest romances, she's just trying to give the world a little more of that. (Okay, maybe a little sexier *that*, but we are now in a new millennium after all.)

A graduate of Wake Forest University, where she met her handsome golf-addicted husband, (who is now sporting dark glasses everywhere he goes) Liz is a mother of two grown sons (also sporting dark glasses) and a miniature Labradoodle named Isabelle. They live in the *Fountain of Youth,* a.k.a. Naples, FL where dancing and romancing continues on ad infinitum.

Visit her website **www.LizKellyBooks.com** for more sneak peeks and to learn about upcoming releases.